HER MATE'S SECRET BABY

INTERSTELLAR BRIDES® PROGRAM - BOOK 9

GRACE GOODWIN

INTERSTELLAR BRIDES® PROGRAM

YOUR mate is out there. Take the test today and discover your perfect match. Are you ready for a sexy alien mate (or two)?

VOLUNTEER NOW!
interstellarbridesprogram.com

GET A FREE BOOK!

JOIN MY MAILING LIST TO BE THE
FIRST TO KNOW OF NEW RELEASES,
FREE BOOKS, SPECIAL PRICES AND
OTHER AUTHOR GIVEAWAYS.

http://freescifiromance.com

CHAPTER 1

N atalie Montgomery, Bride Processing Center, North America

"Keep that stimsphere in your pussy, *gara*."

The voice was deep and commanding and I didn't know what a stimsphere was, nor what *gara* meant. I knew, though, that if I stopped clenching my inner walls around the heavy, solid object, it would fall to the soft rug beneath my bare feet. The round object was inside me, teasing me with what I really wanted… my mate's hard cock.

I closed my eyes, trying to keep the smooth object within. But I was too wet. Too hot. Too ready for my mate to claim me. I knew the ball would fall, and I'd be punished. Again.

The thought made me moan with pleasure, even as a large, warm hand traced the length of my spine from the base of my neck, down over my curves to rest on my bare bottom. Prickly heat stung where I knew he'd spanked me because I let the sphere fall once already. The pressure of it stretching me, filling me, was a carnal tease and my pussy ached for release, ached to tighten around his cock instead. Sweat dripped from my brow as I felt the sphere slip, sensed it at the entrance to my core. About to fall. Not again!

Shifting my hips, I tried to stop the inevitable even as the deep male voice behind me chuckled at my struggle.

"Naughty mate, I see the stimsphere. Hold it inside that wet pussy, or I'll spank you again."

"I... I can't." I was leaning over a small, padded table. I tugged on my arms but realized I was bound to it, ankles and wrists. A cushion was beneath my belly, and while comfortable, I realized I was positioned perfectly for him to do whatever he wanted. My ass was in the air, my bare pussy perfectly exposed for him to see. I could not hide from him.

My mate placed both large hands on my bottom, one on each side, and pulled them apart to inspect me. I'd never been so exposed. So vulnerable.

I expected to feel shame, or embarrassment. But this woman's body reveled in his inspection, knew what would follow.

"You are so wet for me. I understand why you're having trouble, *gara*." His deep voice was rough with his own desire. How I knew that, how I knew exactly how my mate sounded when he was about to lose control and give me what I wanted, I had no idea. But I did. He was close. I just needed to push him. Tempt him.

Shaking with need, I felt cold metal brush against one inner thigh, then the other and knew a heavy chain dangled beneath me, attached to the stimsphere, pulling it slowly, inexorably down.

I was too wet, too aroused, to keep it within. My muscles quivered with the effort to hold it in place, my clit pulsed with the ache and need. But I didn't want the stimsphere, I wanted *him*. Filling me. Stretching me open. Making me come. I opened up, loosened my hold on the sphere and it fell from me and onto the floor.

I gasped, feeling empty. "Please, I need… more."

I didn't even recognize my voice. It was deep and raspy as if I'd been screaming in pleasure. The way I felt, all aching need, I probably hadn't come, but cried out from desperation instead.

This man, my mate, whoever he was, knew how to push me. And I loved it.

He tsked me as I felt his palm stroke over my tender bottom.

"This *is* more, *gara.* Any man could just fuck you, but I am your mate and I know what you need. You need my command, my authority over your body. Only then will you let go."

His hand came down on my bare bottom with a loud crack and I cried out in shock. I knew this wasn't real, that I'd never been spanked before, but whatever *this* was, it hurt, but the pain quickly morphed into a fiery pleasure, merging with the already growing ball of hot, frantic need.

"First you will beg, *gara.* You will lose control. You will forget everything but me." His hot breath fanned my neck just before he kissed me in the sweet spot right behind my ear. "Only then will I fuck you."

"But…"

"This is what you want?" he breathed, as a finger swirled over my entrance.

Oh yes, that was exactly what I wanted. Just the gentlest swipe of that fingertip sent heat clear to my toes. My clit pulsed. "More," I begged.

Pressing his body against mine, I felt every hot, hard inch of him along my back.

"This?" His finger slid inside me. Retreated. "You're dripping for me."

"Please." I clenched my eyes closed, every muscle in my body taut, ready to come like I'd never before in my life.

I just needed a… little… bit… more. I needed him, hard and rough, pulling my hair and rutting into me like he'd never stop. A wildness rose inside me I did not recognize. A desperate, broken cry rose from my throat, the animalistic groan a sound I did not recognize.

"What do you want, *gara?*" He filled me with two fingers and I bit my lip to keep myself from ordering him to fuck me harder. Faster. Deeper. If I tried to hurry his pace, he would leave me dripping and empty until I begged. Cried. Gave him everything.

"You. Please."

His hand retreated and I was empty once again. Wind roared through the top of the tent-like structure and I smelled dry air and leather, almond oil and sand. And my mate. His scent was wild and musky, his unique flavor on my tongue, as if I'd recently had his hard length in my mouth.

God, the thought made me burn. I wanted him. All of him. Everywhere.

I shook my head and sobbed, my hair a silky waterfall that shifted as it hung down over my face. I needed. There was no other word adequate to describe the state of my body. I *needed.*

Somewhere deep within, I knew this had been going on for quite some time. He'd teased me, tormented me with pleasure. But I was beyond the breaking point, cracking open and ready to beg, plead, cry… anything, if he'd just give me his hard…

"Is this what you want?" he said and I felt the hot, round head of his cock align with my entrance.

"Yes." The word exploded from me.

"Do you accept my claim, *gara?* Do you accept my protection and my devotion?"

What the hell was I supposed to say to that? There was only one word running like a chant through my mind, and this body I was in was only too eager to scream it.

"Yes!"

Footsteps. I heard footsteps coming from my right side. I turned my head to see a second pair of boots. Not my mate's. Someone else was here...

"For the official records, have you ever been married, matched, or mated to another man?"

His question slowed my thoughts, cooled my ardor slightly. What, exactly, was going on here? "No."

"Do you have any biological offspring?"

Biological...? "No."

I tensed and tried to pull out of his hands as the booted stranger stepped closer. I could not see his face, but I knew he was here. Knew he could hear my pleas, my pleasure. And, from where he stood, could most likely see my open pussy.

I dropped my forehead to the table with a groan. God, why did that thought turn me on? Had I suddenly become some kind of freak? A pervert?

Before I could dwell on that thought, a gentle hand tangled in my hair at the base of my skull and tugged gently, lifting my head from the table. My back arched and my ass lifted toward his hard cock.

"Good. I claim you as my mate." He thrust forward, filling me in one slow, steady stroke.

The stranger behind me spoke, his voice rough and deep, but easily distinguished from my mate's. "I'll note the official records and alert the council."

"Leave us," my mate ordered, holding himself still deep inside me.

"But, you have not seeded her. Standard protocol dictates I witness—"

"Get out before I cut your cock from your body and shove it down your throat."

I shivered at my mate's rough order. The boots hurried away and I felt a grin spread across my face. My mate was strong. Fierce. Feared. He would not share me.

God, that fucking made me hot.

Riding the edge once more, I wiggled my hips, relieved when he pulled out, then pushed deep. Hard. His hand in my hair pulled my whole body back onto his thick cock. In. Out. Hard. Fast. Rough. Just the way I wanted it. The wet, carnal sounds of fucking filled the tent.

My mate released my hair and bent low, kissing me on the shoulder. His voice was ragged, his breath uneven as he spoke.

"And now, mate, you will know what it means to be mine."

He moved his hand to where I could see a ring on his little finger. My pussy clenched in anticipation. I wondered why for half a second and he pressed the ring's insignia with his thumb.

Vibration exploded in both my nipples and my clit followed with a small shock, like a zinger of electric current.

A scream left my throat as I arched off the table, but my mate grabbed my hips and held me to him, thrusting deeply over and over until the only sound I heard was his body slamming into mine.

Holy shit, it was some kind of remote for... what? Some kind of space vibrator. But on my nipples *and* clit?

Over and over. My nipples sent fire to my core and I exploded, coming so hard I feared I would pass out. My pussy pulsed and clenched around him and I lost control of my body, bucking and writhing like a wild animal as his huge hands held my hips, forced me to take more. My orgasm went on and on, until dizziness swamped me and I couldn't remember where I was.

My mouth was so dry from screaming.

And then things did go black. Sensation faded, as if I were coming out of a dream, a dream I really, really fucking wanted to get back to.

That was the best sex of my life, and I wanted more.

In my experience, waking up always sucked.

"Miss Montgomery?" A stern, female voice called my name.

I shook my head, not wanting to answer. I wanted more of my mate, his hard cock, that incredible orgasm. Holy shit.

"Natalie!" The voice had increased in volume, and now sounded concerned. If I'd learned nothing during my long years of boarding school, I couldn't make myself be rude. Good manners were hard-wired into my system by strict and sometimes ruthless teachers.

"I'm sorry. Yes?" My voice was raspy and weak, as if I'd not used it for days.

"Open your eyes, dear. I need to know you're back here, on Earth, with me."

Reluctantly, I forced my eyes open, the backs of my eyelids like sandpaper. It all rushed back to me. The cold, clinical white walls. The strange chair I was currently strapped into like a demented mental patient. The strange hospital style gown I wore with the Interstellar Brides Processing insignia all over it in a dark burgundy pattern like ugly-ass wallpaper. Even the serious eyes and solemn expression on the pretty brunette woman who was performing my testing. She didn't look like she was much older than me, but the darkness behind her gaze told me she'd lived a hell of a lot more.

Time for me to do some of that thing called life. I was tired of being kept on the shelf like delicate china. I'd cooperated for twenty-four years, and look what that had gotten me. An Ivy League education, parents I never saw more than twice a year, and a fiancé so desperate for hot sex he'd rather pay for it than sleep with me.

True, he'd never rattled my cage like the dream I'd just had, but he hadn't tried all that hard either.

Getting him to eat me out took an act of Congress. He was much more a rut-into-me-like-a-pig-and-walk-away kind of guy. And I'd put up with that for the last eighteen months to try to please my parents. Seriously? What was *wrong* with me?

To make it even worse, the best sex I'd ever had had been a dream. Although, if I was going to get more of that, if I accepted the match, then I was all for it.

"Miss Montgomery, are you with me?"

"Oh, sorry." I blinked a few times and dismissed thoughts of *Curtis Howard Hornsby III* from my mind. Billionaire, silver-spoon, spineless, limp-dicked, cheating low-life. "Yes. I'm here, Warden. Sorry."

"I understand. Take a moment to recover. I know the processing protocol can be intense."

I flushed. "I didn't scream too loudly, did I?"

She smiled, then looked away. "No, not too loudly," she replied, but I didn't believe her. The way I'd come apart in the dream, surely everyone in the processing center had heard me.

"Yeah, about that. Sorry, but it was... God." I couldn't even explain it.

"Yes, I understand." The warden's name was Egara. I remembered that now. But was that her first name? Or last? It was a weird name for a woman, but then, I'd heard rumors from some of the others being processed in the center the last few days that Warden Egara had been mated to not one, but *two* warriors from a planet called Prillon Prime. And they'd both died. She was a double widow.

Sad. It sounded so sad.

Warden Egara looked down at the tablet in her hand, one it seemed she always carried, and nodded briskly. "Excellent. You have a ninety-nine percent match."

"I do?" Yes, that pathetically hopeful voice was mine. My mother would scowl at the unnecessary display of emotion. But screw her, screw my billionaire banker father and their decision to have a child simply to conform to societal expectations. I'd been raised by nannies and housemothers in boarding school. I'd learned to keep a stiff upper lip from the age of three, and I wasn't even British.

As of today, my mother's opinion no longer mattered. I needed to remember that. I was getting off this stupid planet. I was going to have a real life, with a man, an alien, mate, whatever, that was ninety-nine percent matched to me. I didn't care what he was called, as long as he *cared*. For once in my life, I wanted someone to put me first.

That one simple characteristic wasn't my ex-fiancé's or my parents' nature. Hell, their consistent lack of interest in their only daughter probably meant that they wouldn't even realize I was gone until Christmas, which was four months away.

"Yes, Natalie. You've been matched to Trion." The warden's eyes warmed slightly, and I relaxed back into the examination chair. I felt like I was at the dentist, but I wasn't going to bring that up. And I wasn't getting a filling, I was getting a man. A mate. A life.

"Okay." I didn't know anything about the planet, and I didn't care. Anywhere had to be better than Earth, because when my parents and Curtis paid attention, they noticed everything and dictated what I did, what I wore, who I socialized with.

I'd pulled up my big girl panties and rebelled a few times, but that had never worked. It was a new boarding school or a first-class ticket home from wherever I'd run to. Just last year, I'd gone on an Alaskan cruise and was met in Juneau by a Montgomery lackey to retrieve me. It had been a fucking cruise, but that wasn't allowed.

The only way to break free was to leave the planet, to go in a way that they couldn't get me back. I glanced down at my left hand, at the oversized diamond engagement ring still on my finger. When I looked up, it was to see that Warden Egara had been watching me. "Can you take it off?"

With my wrists restrained, it wasn't like I was going to do it. But I wasn't going into space matched to an alien from Trion wearing Curtis' ring. It was big and gorgeous and I didn't want it. I wanted my matched spaceman. "Will you help? I can't reach it."

She nodded and walked to my side. She set the tablet next to my knee and carefully worked the ring from my finger. The moment it was off, I felt a bubbling, giddy sense of freedom. Was I really going to do this, leave everyone and everything?

Yes. Yes, I was. I wiggled my fingers and sighed. "Thank you."

She held the ring and raised a brow. "What do you wish me to do with it?"

"I don't care. Sell it. Keep the money. Give it away. Throw it in the trash. Whatever you want."

"All right." She slid the ring into her pocket and I worried she might actually throw it away.

"It's worth well over thirty-thousand dollars. Don't take a penny less."

Nodding, she reached for the tablet again. She didn't seem impressed by the ring and I liked her all the more for it. It seemed she wanted love over objects, just like me. The ring meant nothing because *I* meant nothing to Curtis. I settled back against the chair.

"For the record, Miss Montgomery, are you now, or have you ever been married?"

"No." These were the same questions I'd been asked before, but I knew this was the last time. Now I had a mate. A match. A man who was supposed to be paired to my psychological profile perfectly. Knowing that my mate waited for me only made the questions seem much more real.

"Have you produced any biological offspring?"

"Hell, no." And before today, I'd never wanted to. Curtis had never inspired me to want a child, and my own upbringing had left me cold. If I ever had a baby, I'd need to take mothering classes or something. I'd have to do all the things my mother never did, like learn all the little songs and games little ones played. The ABCs. I knew the ABCs.

Did they even have an alphabet on Trion? Suddenly, I couldn't wait to find out. I bet it had its own special children's song. I'd learn it right away, and sing it to my baby. Maybe even before it was born. They could hear in there, right? Maybe I'd sing both songs, English and Trion.

Wow. I wanted a baby. That was a new one. Had they given me something during testing to wake up my ovaries?

"Natalie?"

I blinked up at Warden Egara. "Yes."

"I know it's difficult, but try to stay with me. We're almost done. Do you accept the results of the matching protocol?"

"Yes." Oh, hell yes, *gara* accepted. I laughed. I couldn't help it. Elation washed through me, hot and heady. I felt… happy. For once, I had something to be excited about, and I'd done it by myself, for myself. "Sorry, I'm kind of excited."

The warden patted me on the shoulder and walked to the opposite side of the room, her form-fitting gray uniform reminded me of that sexy, alien character, Seven of Nine on

Star Trek. Curtis had always pointed out how sexy that stupid, blonde actress looked in her sparkly, super-tight, silver spacesuit. She was a cyborg on the television show. How was a machine woman sexy? I didn't get it, but Curtis drooled every time she came on the television screen, even if I was sitting right next to him on the couch.

Well, I had the last laugh. Curtis was stuck here, on Earth, paying his *escorts* to suck his dick and living inside that bank eighty hours a week like a robot. I was the one going off on a sexy adventure in space.

God, I hoped my Trion mate was hot. Smoking hot. Drench-my-panties hot, just like the dream.

A bright blue light appeared in the wall to my left and the chair lurched sideways.

Startled, I looked up to see Warden Egara smiling at me. "Try to relax. All planets have specifications for their mates. All modifications for Trion will be made as part of your processing. When you wake up, you'll be on Trion. You will no longer be a citizen of Earth. Your new mate will be waiting."

I leaned back, ready for whatever insanity was about to happen. Actually, I was simply trying not to throw up.

I was leaving home. Forever. I'd read the handbook. I knew what I was getting into and knew I couldn't come back. But thinking and doing were two separate things.

When the giant needle thing came at me, I flinched. When it stabbed me just behind my ear, near the temple, I tried to ignore the pain as the warden explained they were implanting neural processors to help me learn the Trion language.

Cool.

The chair lowered me into a warm, blue bath and a feeling of calm settled over me. I figured they were drugging me and I didn't care. At least I wasn't about to lose my cookies all over this glamorous hospital gown.

"Your processing will begin in three... two... one." Warden Egara gave a little wave as the wall slid closed behind me.

And then...nothing.

ouncilor Roark, Outpost Two, Southern Continent, Planet Trion

"Councilor!"

I turned at the voice and looked between the two tents waiting for the owner of that deep voice to appear. The two suns made for a hot, bright day and I did not have proper cover to linger outside. The young man who ran toward me in the sand was newly assigned to my personal guard detail. He was my cousin's son, eager and loyal, even if he was barely over twenty summers. "What is it, Byran?"

True, he was young, but his body shook with a mixture of eagerness and excitement "She's here!"

When I frowned, he continued, "Your female. The alien from Earth."

My back went straight and the breath left my body as if I'd been punched in the stomach. "My mate is here?" I asked. "The transport was to occur when the first sun set." I scanned the sky in less than a second. "I did not expect her for half a day."

While he stood at attention before me, as was appropriate considering my rank, he shrugged. "I do not know the details, Councilor, but she is here. I saw her." A look something akin to longing crossed over his face.

"Is she beautiful?" I shouldn't ask him. For what could he say? No, sir, she's hideous? Of course not. Even if it were truth.

"She's incredible, Councilor. I've never seen a woman who looks like her."

I walked with haste to the small transport station, which was as temporary and rustic as the entire outpost. Here for only a few days to meet with tribal leaders in the area, I'd been shocked when the Interstellar Brides Program notified me of my mate's pending arrival. Even my parents rushed from their comfortable and lavish home in the capital city of Xalia to meet her, the future of our family, the woman who would bear my children.

Pushing back the flap of the tent, I ducked to fit through the entry and took in the small group of men. Standing in a semicircle, they looked down at the ground at something, which I assumed was my mate.

It had been more than a month since I'd submitted to the Interstellar Brides Program's matching protocols. I did not remember much of the test itself. I'd fallen asleep and woken with my heart racing, a raging cock and a feeling of complete satisfaction. I had no idea what type of female I would be assigned, nor did I care. I simply wanted her to arrive. Ruling was a lonely job, and as much as I admired and respected my parents, they were cold comfort when I lay in bed at night. Alone.

Yes, there were Trion females aplenty more than eager to

ride my cock, but they all wanted something in return. Wealth. Status. Power.

But the female who had just arrived would want nothing more than my dominant hand on her body and my cock buried deep...

Clearing my throat, the men turned and bowed. Transport centers on Trion were, by necessity, mobile, their location kept secret. The rebellious faction of Drovers on the southern continent were aggressive and determined. The Drovers wanted Trion to abandon our oath to the Interstellar Coalition, to send no more soldiers, no more brides. The Drovers believed our technology and stubborn tribal blood would be enough to protect us from the Hive scourge.

They were wrong. I'd seen what was out there, in space. I'd been on the front lines of the war. I'd served four years, as was required from all Trion volunteers. And I knew, beyond any shadow of a doubt, that the Drover factions were wrong.

The Hive would conquer us in a matter of weeks without the protection of the Interstellar Fleet.

Still, some refused to believe the truth. Because of this, the Transport Outposts were moved often, their location kept secret from all but a few. As a result, I came to be in the middle of the desert at Outpost Two, the nearest transport station available out here in the wilds of the southern continent. I was content in the capital, surrounded by loyal guards and advisors, away from the complications and maneuverings a visit to the outposts always brought about. At home, I could be with my people, lead and rule them effectively. Here, I was constantly on guard, every word from my mouth had the potential to start a skirmish between tribes, a battle over resources, water or women. One hint of weakness was all it would take to destabilize the region.

I was never weak.

Here, councilors from all over Trion would meet, those

meetings often dragging out for days of rituals, ass-kissing and bargaining.

I had come to Outpost Two for such a meeting, but as soon as I knew my mate would arrive, I'd done what I could to keep a low profile, waiting for my mate. Waiting, and imagining what she might look like. How hot her pussy would feel wrapped around my cock. I could almost hear the soft cries of her pleasure as I took her from behind on the claiming bench, over and over again.

Three days of waiting.

Now, the wait was over. She was here and I could make her mine and take her home. Finally.

I didn't say anything, just crossed the space and the men parted, allowing me, at last, to see my mate.

My eyes widened at her sleeping form. Her *naked* sleeping form. Her body was ripe with curves, full, lush breasts led to a tapered waist. Her skin was pale, no doubt untouched by the harsh desert suns. Her hair shimmered softly in the light cast by a half dozen lamps surrounding the transport platform. None had dared touch her, but I studied her softness against the dark gray surface of the transport and worried that the journey had injured her. Why was she not awake?

I stepped closer, crouched down in front of her and studied her delicate features. Her lips were pink and full. Her face tapered to a slightly pointed chin that I ached to kiss. Her golden hair looked as if it had been woven with strips of pure gold from Trion's many mines.

She was stunning and I struggled with thought as my body reacted to her beauty. No wonder Byran had lust in his eyes.

No doubt, they all did. The men surrounding me. Suddenly, I became all too aware of their continued presence.

Fark!

Looking about, I yanked a long robe from one of the men's arms and draped it over my mate, ensuring her gorgeous body was completely covered. Only her head and neck were exposed. Turning my head, I looked up at the men, who now looked abashed and nervous.

"That is my mate you have been ogling," I said, my voice sharp and cold. "Since you were looking at her *naked* body, I assume you saw the disks that indicated she has a master?"

Everyone's eyes lowered to the ground.

"Not one of you thought to cover her? Not one of you thought of her modesty, that she is mine? That her body is solely for my pleasure, not yours?"

My voice raised with each word and the last question was shouted. Everyone in camp must have heard me.

I stood to my full height and crossed my arms over my chest.

"Byran!"

The young man stepped forward, shoulders back, chin up. "Yes, Councilor?"

"Find the doctor and bring her here. Immediately."

"And your parents?"

Fark. I'd forgotten them in the surprise. They'd journeyed to the outpost to meet my mate. Eager for me to continue the line of Trion leaders with the next generation, they'd pressured me to take a bride, a political match. As the dutiful son, I'd allowed them to parade women before me for months. My position as councilor ensured I could have chosen almost any bride from the capital, but I found I did not enjoy their calculating looks or false humility. They were women born to powerful families, pampered and protected. Arrogant and entitled. When my mother insisted I choose one of them, I'd refused, and my father, for once, had taken my side against his mate. He understood my desire for a woman all my own. He wanted for me what he had enjoyed these last years, a true mate, one perfectly matched to me, as my mother had been to him. And so, I'd attempted to please my parents, my agreeing to take a mate, but one of my own choosing. One matched to me. A perfect match.

I looked to Byran, who waited patiently, his hands clasped in front of his waist.

"Yes, alert them of her arrival." As much as I wanted to meet my bride alone, I knew that was not possible. Not here, at Outpost Two. We'd be swarmed with curious eyes, my mother's at the front of the line.

Byran knew nothing of my inner turmoil. I kept my face carefully blank as he bowed and dashed off.

"As for the rest of you…. out!" I yelled.

The remaining onlookers scurried through the opening in the tent and while I heard them murmuring as they fled, I didn't listen, for my attention was on my mate before me.

She was asleep. She wasn't dead, since I could see the slight rise and fall of the robe. I would not leave her on the hard transport deck, so I scooped her up into my arms and carried her over to a chair. I felt no strain lifting her; Earth females seemed to be quite small. I remembered the High Councilor's mate, Eva, who was also a wisp of a female in comparison to her master, Tark. Sitting down with her tucked against me on my lap, I sighed loudly, allowed my frustration and anger to seep from me now that I finally had her in my arms.

My mate was warm and soft and I leaned down to brush my face over her soft hair. Silky and the prettiest color. Breathing in her scent, I closed my eyes. This was my mate! Out of the entire universe, she was my perfect match. I was confident in her, even though she had yet to open her eyes. She was mine. I had my parents and one sister to whom I was dedicated, but having a mate call me master was something else entirely. I felt possessiveness swirl through my veins.

A female a decade older than my thirty summers came through the entry, then bowed. She wore the uniform of a Trion doctor and carried a small bag. Inside would be all that was needed to diagnose, treat and heal most illnesses, wounds and injuries. "Councilor, I heard your mate has been transported. Congratulations. Do you wish me to fully examine her for mating?"

"No. I wish for you to inform me of her general health, Doctor." I shifted her so I could stroke my hand over her hair. I wanted to feel it beneath my palm, to touch her. "The mating tests, however, I will perform myself. I have found I am a little...protective where my mate is concerned."

"Yes, I heard of your unhappiness with regards to the others." I could hear her own displeasure in her tone. "Then you do not wish for this exam to be witnessed by someone other than myself, for the official records?"

"*Fark*, no." The answer was instant and almost feral. Enough of the outpost had seen her naked already.

"You are aware that it is standard protocol for you to claim her before an official witness, and for the event to be recorded for the brides program's system monitors."

I tightened my hold on my mate. The thought of one of those overeager asses watching me fill this small female with my seed did not appeal. No one would hear her cries of surrender, of pleasure, but me. "I am aware of the tradition. I simply choose not to honor it. I assure you, Doctor, that I will fuck my mate more than once. There will be ample opportunity for the brides program's monitors to record the activity."

I saw the corner of her mouth tip up, but she did not comment on the subject any further. I was the Councilor of the southern fucking continent. If anyone wanted to ensure my mate was well and truly mated, they could just look at her face tomorrow. It would have the glow of a well-fucked female. That was all these bastards at this outpost were going to get. They were a bunch of horny heathens and I would not allow them to satisfy their curiosity or hunger for female flesh with my mate.

"If I may look at her?"

"Yes, Doctor," I replied, loosening my hold. While a female doctor was not the norm, I was pleased she was stationed to this outpost, for I could not tolerate having another male look at her, even with the most clinical of intents.

"Would you prefer to hold her as I scan her, or place her on the table?"

Her deference was appreciated and I would assist her in any way I could to strengthen her position among the medical elite back home. She was being supportive of me and my needs with regards to my mate. I could support her. "Do it here."

She nodded, then knelt before me. Meeting my gaze for a moment, she found the edges of the robe and parted it. I'd had only the briefest glimpses of my mate before I covered her. She'd been on her side, her legs bent, but I hadn't missed the curve of her hip, her pale skin, her full breasts, the thin gold chain that dangled between her nipples, anchored in the piercing on each pink tip. The processing center on Earth did an excellent job with the modifications required for Trion. With her in my lap, I could take my time and look my fill. Her breasts were a handful, the nipples a pale blush color. With the golden rings through them, the tips were tightly furled. I recognized my seal embossed on the gold medallions affixed to the chain. The sight pleased me greatly, my most primitive need to announce to the planet exactly who this female belonged to was assuaged. No one would question her identity or my claim. Her abdomen was slightly curved and she was bare above her pussy, although, with her legs together and bent, I could see nothing more.

I grew hard as I imagined what awaited me between those soft, supple thighs.

The doctor took a ReGen wand from her bag and slowly moved it across my mate's body from head to feet and back again. The doctor's eyes remained on the sensors and colored lights as she did so.

"Roark, we heard she has arrived." My father's voice filled the small area inside the tent and I lifted my gaze to find my parents entering without my leave. Until this moment, their arrogance had never bothered me. But now, I found a deep-seated rage boiling just below the surface at their intrusion.

"Yes, Father."

The doctor must have seen the tightness in my jaw, for she quickly reached over and pulled the robe back over my mate's body.

He stepped forward but I shook my head and my mother reached out to stop him with a small hand on his arm. "Congratulations, son."

"My thanks, Mother." I'd always been told I looked just like my father. Tall, broad shouldered, black hair, equally black eyes. His was threaded with streaks of silver. I had a close-cut beard, while he was clean-shaven. Still, look like him, I did. But it was my mother's cunning, her cold-blooded and mercenary logic when it came to policy decisions, that I shared. She'd been my father's constant, and loving, companion and most trusted advisor for many decades. He'd served as Councilor over the southern continent for twenty years before stepping aside in favor of me. As had happened for generations, I was immediately voted in as his replacement.

Refusing the role, the duty and heavy responsibilities that

came with it, had never been an option. I'd been raised from birth to serve my people. I respected my role, and my family's honor. Tradition. My sister's mate served as second for the High Councilor of Trion. Our family was dedicated to service. I'd never wanted anything for myself. I'd never been allowed.

But the woman in my arms was *mine*, and I found, for the first time in my life, I resented my parents intrusion into what should have been something private and sacred. My mate. She knew nothing of Trion politics, of my family's elite status on the planet, of our wealth and massive military power. The Interstellar Brides Program matching protocols had paired us as perfect for one another as a man and a woman.

I'd finally bed a woman I knew wanted me with no ulterior motives or political aspirations. She was mine. The thought made my cock hard and my heart ache. Pain radiated up from my chest to my throat as I looked down at my mate's gentle face. Still, she slept. Her long, pale lashes rested in elegant perfection on her high cheekbones. Her nose was straight and smooth, her brows arched delicately above eyes I could not wait to see.

Were they golden? Dark brown? Or fair and strange, like her beautiful golden hair and skin?

My mother had entered first and stepped closer to peer down at her. "She is quite small. Why is she covered so?"

CHAPTER 3

I DID NOT WISH to disrespect my mother, but I had to share my plans for my mate as I intended to proceed. "She is covered, Mother, because I wish it."

"But I wish to see her, to see the female who will give me grandchildren."

My mother wore the simple garb of those from the southern continent, although the material of her dress was quite fine.

"You will have decades to see her, Mother. Just not naked."

The doctor glanced up at me, then back down at the ground, knowing this conversation was not for her.

"Where are the others?" She looked around as if the men were hiding somewhere. "Someone must observe the mating."

My back stiffened. "I assure you, Mother, it will not be

you. Please leave so the doctor can continue her examination."

My father placed a hand on her shoulder and she glanced to him, just as she always did.

"I understand your possessiveness, but I will not have anyone doubt the match, son. You know the other regions. They are much more traditional."

There was no way either of my parents were going to watch me fuck my mate.

"She is not of Trion and does not know our ways. Mother, would you like to be transported to Earth, arrive naked, and submit to a mate you'd never met before? With witnesses?"

She pursed her lips but did not respond.

"It would be difficult for you to perform."

I would have laughed at the ridiculous humor of my father's words, for I would have no problem fucking my mate. Both my parents forgot that this wasn't a Trion match, even though it had been their idea. This was a brides program testing match. The compatibility percentage on every aspect of a pairing was so high that even my parents' decades-long union couldn't compare.

"But—"

"Mother. I am Councilor of the southern continent, not your son in this moment. I need you to go with Father and leave me with my mate. Once I am done here, I am going to the oasis, to Mirana for the night. I will not mate her here." I glanced at my mother. "The wait is over. You have seen her for yourself, so there is no reason to remain. Please take the transport back to Xalia. We will follow you tomorrow just as soon as I have completed the mating, then spend the week with you. I look forward to it."

Both of my parents nodded, albeit reluctantly, and left the tent. They didn't bow as was required, for while I'd just said I was to be treated as their ruler, they saw me as their son first.

"Continue, Doctor," I said. I was relieved to know my parents were content with my mate's arrival and even more so that they were gone. I didn't need them about when I had a new mate.

She offered a nod as she parted the robe again and continued her test. Once finished, she returned the tool to her bag, then met my eyes.

"She is well. The High Councilor's mate was also from Earth and the sensors have been calibrated for humans and the stress of transporting such a distance. They indicate for a human her heart rate, blood pressure, brain wave function, and motor skills are all in working order. She has no detectable deficiencies and no diseases or illnesses were indicated on the scan."

I sighed, relieved. She wasn't even awake and I was protective.

"Then why does she not awaken?"

"I have not met someone who has transported such a distance, only those across the planet. Therefore, based on her test results, I assume the trip was just taxing. Earth is many light years away."

She did have a valid point. My mate was quite small and making the journey *would* be tiring. I was just anxious for her to be awake so I knew she truly was healthy after what she endured. Besides, I wanted to know her eye color.

"You will need to perform the remainder of the standard mating tests yourself, specifically the neurostim exam," the doctor added.

My cock hardened against my mate's side at the thought.

The doctor stood and picked up her bag, pulling out the neurostim tool, showing it to me, then placing it on the nearby table. "You will wish to ensure she is safe to breed and responsive to sexual stimuli."

"She is my mate. I am confident that she will be responsive, for I am eager for her." I took a moment to study the doctor. "You were mated, Doctor?"

I used the past tense, for I sensed that was no longer the case. She was one of my people and I could read them well. It was my job to do so. As I was used to being alone, I'd had to learn that skill at an early age.

The doctor met my eyes. "Yes. It was a good match, but he was killed by the Hive. I understand your instant possessiveness and appreciate your... conscientiousness toward her. I remember first meeting him to be a little scary and my mate was only from the northern continent. For her—" she tilted her head toward my mate, "—as you told your parents, it will be twice as difficult."

I offered the doctor a small smile. "Then it is good that I am twice as obsessed, twice as possessive."

"Yes, it is, although I am sure she will not be well versed in our ways. She may resist you."

"Then she will learn." The unforgiving councilor roared to life within me before I could temper him. But the doctor only chuckled.

"We shall see. She will awaken soon. Just be patient until then."

"Thank you, Doctor."

She bowed and left.

I was alone with my mate, and the medical device I knew would bring her much pleasure. Parting the robe again, I looked my fill, shifting her so that I could stroke my knuckles over her soft, warm skin. The touch was not sexual and she was not completely bare to me, although my cock did rise at the feel of her, all too eager to caress, to touch, to explore my mate's body. I was in awe of this female. She was mine. Every inch of her was perfect. Just for me.

While I knew my parents loved me, they were overly attentive. I'd been born with a father as councilor and grew up familiar with leadership and the civic-minded responsibility expected of me. I never considered another role other than taking over from my father at his retirement. This one-mindedness and strong parental support allowed for me to climb through the ranks in the government. My drive had been singular and I became the planet's youngest councilor. Needless to say, my parents had been thrilled and did everything in their power to keep the leadership of our part of the planet under our family's strong supervision. But the role of councilor was… well, lonely. I had yet to find a Trion mate and my parents had become concerned. That was why I now held an Earth female in my lap. All reservations melted away from the heat of her in my arms.

She stirred, moaned, blinked once, then again. Her blue— *blue!*—eyes met mine, but she didn't truly see me. Not until her body stiffened and she sat up, almost hitting my chin with her forehead.

"Easy, *gara*."

"Who… who are you?" Her voice was soft and tentative. Delicate.

"I am Roark, your mate."

"Roark." Her eyes widened and I forgot to blink when she focused them on me. Such a color I had never seen before. Blue, as pale blue as frozen ice in a glacier, and clear as a cloudless sky. The people of Trion were darker by nature, dark of hair and eye. Her exotic beauty, pale blue eyes and golden hair, would make her much coveted by all who saw her. While she attempted to relax, I could sense her nervousness.

"It worked," she commented.

"What?"

"The transport." She nodded, her head rubbing against my chest with the slight movement. "Am I on Trion then?"

"You are. We are at Outpost Two in the southern continent. What is your name?"

"Natalie. Natalie Montgomery."

Natalie.

"Do you feel well, Natalie Montgomery?"

She took a moment, as if thinking about each part of her body. "Yes."

"Good. Then I can perform the remainder of the medical tests."

"Remainder?" she wondered.

"Yes, you slept through the doctor's initial scans and she assured me you are well, but there are a few others that must be done now that you awake."

She struggled to sit up, so I assisted, but did not allow her off my lap. When the robe slipped off a shoulder and exposed one breast, she gasped.

Her hand moved to cover herself, but I stilled her action with one of mine. "Do not hide yourself from me."

"I'm naked!" she said, stating the obvious, then frowned. Pulling the robe away from her body, she peeked down at herself, then up at me. "I… I have nipple rings!"

I couldn't help but smile at the look of utter surprise on her face. "Females on Earth are not adorned by their mates?"

"Um, a few."

I made a sound of agreement. "Mated Trion females have nipple rings. As my mate, you are also adorned with gold, and with my chain, which marks you clearly as mine."

"Chain?"

I removed her hand from her robe and the garment dropped to her waist. She looked down and gasped. I picked up the delicate gold chain that dangled and swung, perfectly displayed between her nipples and held it up so she could see the string of small disks woven into the links. Every small gold disk was embossed with the mark of my family. "This symbol is the mark of your new family, mate. You are mine, and this adornment ensures all who see you will know exactly who you belong to."

"I don't want to be tagged like a stray dog, like I'm property."

It was my turn to frown. "What is this *stray dog?* You are not a stray, Natalie. You are the matched mate of a councilor. You will be treated with respect and reverence. None will dare insult or belittle you. You are mine, and under my protection."

"Wow. Are you for real?" She looked up at me, and the crystal blue of her eyes shocked me with their intensity.

"I am very real. And you are mine to adorn, mine to protect. You need not fear ever again. I will take care of you, Natalie. You are the most important thing on this planet to me now. You have my solemn vow." I lifted my hand to her cheek, unable to release her gaze from my own. I wanted her to look upon me for a bit longer. As I stroked her cheek with the softest touch I could manage, I wondered what her eyes would look like clouded with desire. Trust. Love.

She was the one to look away. "I'm just...I don't know. Not used to having a chain dangling from my nipples."

"You do not wish to be marked as mine? To let everyone on Trion know who you belong to, who is your master?"

"My... my master?" Hearing that word fall from her lips made my cock swell uncomfortably in my pants. I wanted to hear her chant the word, preferably as I thrust into her wet heat. No, I wanted her to scream it.

"I am yours, Natalie. Always. As you are mine. Do you not have some kind of sign of mating on Earth?"

"A ring." She paused, then continued. "On your finger.

Here." She pointed to her left hand, then at her breasts. "Not here."

I did not wish to continue this vein of conversation. I was not removing the nipple rings, nor the chain. Ever.

I stood then, keeping her in my arms, and walked over to the table. While it wasn't an exam table, the height worked perfectly as one. I sat her down on the edge and slowly, gently pushed the robe from her shoulders until it fell next to her hips on the table. Eager to know what it would feel like to be in her arms, I maneuvered her legs, parting them and stepping forward to stand between her knees.

Natalie looked up at me with shock and uncertainty in her eyes, but I saw something else there as well. Curiosity? Desire? Hope?

Hope seemed a strange thing in the moment, but I dismissed it and leaned forward to press my forehead to hers. "I must complete the doctor's examination now, mate."

"I can't believe I slept through a doctor's exam." Her breath tickled my lower lip and I nearly groaned.

"Yes. Doctor Karran was here, but I asked her to leave us alone."

"Why? You said I wasn't sick. Is something wrong with me?" With the robe settled about her waist, only her hips and pussy were covered. Otherwise, she was bare. Her embarrassment, if she'd had any, was forgotten because I'd frightened her with my careless words.

"No, mate. No. I did not allow her to complete all of the tests on your body."

"Why not?"

I touched her then because I had to, because I could no longer resist temptation. Settling my hands at her waist, I lowered my lips to her cheek and kissed her. Once. Twice. More. She was addictive. "Because I could not bear to have another see you, or witness your pleasure."

"Pleasure? What are you talking about?" Natalie was confused, but my patience was at an end.

"Lie down on the table, mate. The sooner I complete the medical exam, the sooner we can go. I have a surprise for you."

 *atalie*

HOLY EFFING HELL. Roark was *mine?* Was this a cosmic joke? He stood before me, looming, all protective and growly and bossy, and I could do nothing but stare and wonder what drug I'd taken.

This couldn't be real. He was too perfect to be real.

His clothes didn't scream *alien.* His pants and boots were simple and black. He wore an odd gray tunic that highlighted every huge bulge of muscle on his massive chest and shoulders. He looked human, just a bit bigger than I was used to. He made Curtis, with his stringy blond hair, skinny torso and loafers, look like a twelve-year-old boy. Roark was *all* man. His hair was so dark it looked black, his eyes were focused and intense, the color of espresso. And his voice? It gave me shivers. So deep. So commanding. God, I wanted him to talk dirty to me in that voice.

Fuck me, Natalie.

You like that, naughty girl?

Oh, good grief. What the hell was wrong with me?

I transported halfway across the galaxy and woke up horny?

Yes. Apparently, that was exactly what happened. But was it me, or *him*?

So effing hot.

"Lie down on the table, mate. The sooner I complete the medical exam, the sooner we can go. As I said, I have a surprise for you." Roark's lips grazed my cheek and I responded to him automatically, lying down on my back on the hard table. He tugged at the robe bunched under my hips and I lifted my bottom off the table as he pulled it free and tossed the soft fabric to the ground, forgotten.

I licked my lips and tried to lie still, but it was difficult. I was naked and tried not to fidget or act weird. Nope. Nothing weird about this. I lay down naked on a table on an alien world before an Adonis and waited for some kind of freaky medical exam. No big deal. *Yeah, right.*

"Good, Natalie." Roark nodded his approval and I felt like a little kid who just received a gold star on a test. He stepped to the side and retrieved an oddly shaped object from a nearby stand. Returning, he stood on my right. His left hand settled gently on my right thigh. His right hand held aloft the weird medical thing as he looked down at me. "Are you ready, mate?"

I could feel the frown crinkle my forehead, then smoothed it quickly, remembering my mother said that action would give me wrinkles.

"What are you going to do?" Not that I had any choice, apparently, but I wanted to know.

"I'm going to test your body's reaction to stimuli, and ensure that you are fertile and able to accept my seed and make it grow."

"What?" I jerked upright but his hand settled on my chest, just above my breasts, pushing me back down. The chain swung and brushed against my belly.

"The testing is required."

I felt my eyes widen as I studied the device in his hand more closely. It looked like a large dildo with a couple of crazy attachments. I did not approve of the direction my imagination was going with this one. "And what are you going to do with that thing, exactly?"

He held me down, but his smile was pure male satisfaction. "I'm going to fuck you with it, and make you come so the doctor will know your body functions as a proper mate's should."

"You're out of your mind. That's not medical," I replied, sputtering at the insanity of his plan.

He tilted his head as if I'd insulted him. Seriously? He was serious about this?

"You do not wish to cooperate with the exam?"

"We don't have exams like this on Earth. This is crazy and definitely not necessary."

"You are on Trion now. Planetary law and custom demands you be tested. If you are not suitable, I will be forced to request another female."

That stopped me cold. No. This man was mine. He'd promised me already. The match had been made and I was *not* going back. I wasn't going to let a stupid probe thing ruin this.

Besides, maybe it would be just like my battery operated boyfriend back home. Heaven only knew how many times I'd had to resort to B-O-B when Curtis was too busy, or too tired, to take me to bed. "All right. Fine," I grumbled. I was naked. I had nipple rings. He stood between my spread thighs. Perhaps he could make me come. Curtis certainly couldn't. I sighed. "Just get it over with."

I relaxed under his hand and he smiled, heat simmering in his gaze. "This will be the last time you think that way about me putting something in your pussy."

Oh my.

"Don't try to get up once the test has begun. Don't resist it."

The urge to roll my eyes was strong, but I held back. Barely. "I'll try to hold still."

So, yeah, I thought I'd be able to deal with this. I was so wrong, right from the start.

Roark lifted his hand from my chest and returned it to my thigh. His touch, while rough with callouses, was gentle and warm. "Open your legs for me. Let me see what's mine."

That demanding, guttural voice shouldn't turn me on, but it did. I wasn't Natalie from Earth. He didn't know anything about me, about my life on Earth. Here, on Trion, I could be whatever I wanted. Start again. The first thing I wanted was a man, a real man. Roark's commanding tone, his very demanding tone had me bending my knees slightly and letting my legs fall wide. I couldn't resist teasing him. The very naughty woman I'd always dreamed of being was definitely coming out to play. For him, at least.

I watched his face for a reaction, and was not disappointed. His nostrils flared, as if he wanted to breathe in the scent of my arousal. His hand tightened on my thigh and he stepped to his right to get a better look. I glanced down at my body, unsurprised to see that my pussy was now hairless. The nipple rings tugged and pulled gently on my breasts at the oddest times, making me more aware of them than ever. When Warden Egara said I'd be prepared and then transported, she hadn't been kidding.

Roark set the medical probe down between my legs. I expected him to push it inside me, but instead he set it down on the table between my legs where I could not see it and slid his finger inside me instead.

"You are not wet enough for the probe, Natalie. Your body is not ready."

His finger moved around inside me, as if he were exploring. It felt amazing, but it wasn't going to be enough to make me come. He was light years away from making me come.

"Sorry." I resorted to my old standard, to apologize for being frigid in bed. Curtis said I was difficult, a cold fish. Maybe he was right.

Roark shook his head and inserted a second finger into my body. "Hush, mate. Let me see to you." He bent down and took my nipple into his mouth as he fucked me with two blunt fingers. My nipple was so sensitive, perhaps due to the ring, that I arched up off the table at the first touch of his tongue on the hardened peak. Why it wasn't hurting after being newly pierced, I had no idea. Of course, the thought of being transported across the universe was a little mind bending, too, so two rings in my nipples were perhaps nothing.

"Roark." I buried my fingers in his hair and held him to me, saying his name to ground myself, to remind myself of what was really happening here. Roark was mine. My mate, and starting with his mouth on my nipple, my lover. Finally, I would have someone who *wanted* me. Who wanted to be with me. Who would spend time with me and put me first in his life. My mate.

I was so distracted by Roark's mouth I couldn't focus on his fingers, until they were gone. The cold, blunt tip of the medical probe took their place at the opening of my pussy.

He released my nipple with a small, wicked popping noise and scooted down the table so he could see what he was doing between my legs. With just his mouth on my breast, I was so turned on. I didn't care anymore that this was some kind of medical test. I just wanted it over with so I could get out of here, get my mate alone, and claim him properly. Wow, I felt more from just getting to third base with Roark than all the time I had endured fucking Curtis.

Feeling full of feminine power, I lifted my legs and grabbed my knees with my hands, spreading myself wide for his inspection. "Am I ready yet?"

Roark's response was to push the medical probe inside me, slowly, one huge inch at a time. It was a little bigger than my B-O-B back home, but so good. I closed my eyes and moaned when the probe bottomed out inside me, the odd attachment on the top of the thing hovered over my clit.

"Does that feel all right, Natalie?"

I wasn't sure if he was serious, medically speaking, or talking dirty, so I told him the truth. This was the strangest medical device ever, but I wasn't complaining. If this were what going to the doctor was like on Earth, more people would go. "Yes."

He chuckled as an odd whirring sensation started inside my body. He lowered his head to my nipple again, his hand still on my thigh like liquid heat pouring through me. I was so turned on I didn't know what to do, what to think.

My mate. Roark was my mate. Perfect for me. Apparently, my body knew it.

From inside my pussy, the odd probe heated, the warmth spread like tingles through my entire abdomen, and even to the inside of my ass. I was suddenly burning up, so hot I needed to move. I needed his mouth on my clit, or his hand, or his cock stroking me off. I *needed.*

"Holy shit, Roark!" My back arched as a strong pulse went through my body from my pussy to my clit. It was like lightning, from the inside.

"What the hell is this thing?" I gasped.

"Come for me, mate. Give me everything. I want to watch you lose control."

"Oh!" I twisted my hips from side to side until Roark's heavy hand landed on my mound, not to stroke my clit, but to hold me down. I whimpered, desperate for something more.

The probe thing beeped and my gaze flew to Roark's. His eyes were dark with anticipation as the whirring inside me grew stronger. Another pulse zapped my clit, more intense this time, but when I bucked up off the table, Roark's strong hand held me trapped in place. I couldn't move, couldn't get away. I couldn't escape his strength, his gaze, or the searing pleasure making me lose control of my own body from the inside.

Another beep, faster and higher than the last and I gasped as a strong electrical surge pulsed through the walls of my pussy to my ass. The walls of my core pulsed and clenched down on the thing, which seemed to make it pulse stronger. The wave of sensation continued, as if traveling along my nerve endings like cars on a highway, directly to my clit.

Pulse after pulse rocked me. With Roark looming over me, with no control, I shattered into a million pieces with the most intense orgasm I'd ever had in my life.

My body shivered uncontrollably as Roark bent over, covering my face with gentle kisses. Somehow, I'd pleased him, and that knowledge made me feel oddly happy.

Ten minutes on an alien planet and I'd lost my mind. Lost control of my body, my orgasms. Or, perhaps, ten minutes with my new mate. I closed my eyes and allowed him to comfort me as the strange device in my pussy quieted until I could feel nothing but a small, almost imperceptible hum.

"You are so beautiful when you come." Roark whispered the words against my lips, but I was not ready to kiss him. Not yet. Not lying here like a freakish sexual science experiment. He nudged at my lips with his own, but I turned my head slightly so his kiss landed on the corner of my mouth, not the center. While it had been the hottest thing I'd ever done, it was still with a device, not Roark.

He kissed me anyway and gently removed the device from my body, looked down at it. "The readings say that you are fertile for breeding and that you will be receptive to my seed."

Receptive? If that was what it would always be like, or better since I'd get Roark's cock instead of a medical device, then I'd definitely be receptive.

"What now?" I stared at the side of the strange wall as I tried to catch my breath. We were in some kind of tent. Odd that I hadn't noticed it before now. The scent of almonds, or almond oil filled the air, and it was warm. Not uncomfortably so, but a far cry from Boston in January.

"Now, mate, I will take you to our private retreat where I will fuck your sweet pussy until you scream my name, until there is no doubt in your heart or mind exactly whom you belong to."

CHAPTER 5

oark

OUTPOST TWO WAS CREATED at first because of the oasis, travelers using it as a destination for its beauty in the middle of the barren desert. Also for its lifesaving properties of water and shade from the two suns and endless desert. That the outpost grew in place around it was to my advantage that Natalie had transported here, for the oasis was the perfect place to take her to be alone. My tent, while private, had the same thin walls as all the others and no sounds could be muffled. Natalie had screamed when she came all over the probe and I knew everyone could hear. That couldn't be helped since the medical testing had to be done. It was the only time I would allow others to hear her pleasure.

I had discovered, since her arrival, a darkly possessive streak that I'd never before wrestled to control. I wanted all of her, her secrets, her body, her pleasure, to be mine and mine alone.

The others at the outpost would believe the doctor had completed the testing, and once completed, that Natalie's uninhibited scream so soon after was from my claiming, her first hard fucking. The sounds of her pleasure would satisfy anyone who doubted our match. None would dare argue that I'd not completed the protocols or requirements for claiming a new mate. Even my parents would not dare protest.

I wanted to claim my mate in secret. I didn't want the entire outpost listening, nor my mother, father, or any number of ambassadors or tribal leaders watching. No one would see her beautiful body, her pink pussy, her flushed skin when I made her come all over my cock. This would be special. I wanted her cries of pleasure when she came by my cock or my fingers or mouth just for me. Always just for me.

While I'd led Natalie across the outpost with guards following, they remained outside the oasis, maintaining our safety and their distance. I was thankful my parents had left me alone with her, returning to Xalia as I instructed. But I knew that upon our arrival in the city, they would wish to meet her, teach her everything it meant to be a councilor's mate. Before then, I wanted to learn the real Natalie, the one without any knowledge of Trion, no artifice, no guile. Just her.

"What is this place?" Natalie asked, looking all around, wide eyed, as I held her hand and led her down a narrow path.

I tried to see the thick foliage as she did. Lush leaves surrounded us in a splash of color, deep reds, purples and brown of the native plants hung overhead in a giant canopy that blocked the intense rays of Trion's twin suns. There was a deep pool of water in the center that fed all the growth and it was actually humid, a rarity on Trion. Beneath our feet, sand was replaced by dark brown moss and loam, rich and moist. Sounds of moving water and animals were almost noisy after only the blowing wind through the tents.

"This is Mirana, an oasis. It was discovered thousands of years ago and was how people survived when crossing the desert. There were no transport stations and so the nomads walked and sought shelter here. Water. Sustenance."

"We have such places as well," she commented, touching a large leaf. I was not an expert on foliage, for trees were rare, but I knew none were poisonous and I doubted she would pick one and eat it. Although, she was from Earth and I didn't know their customs or plant life. I'd have to watch her closely, or perhaps distract her from the possibility with more carnal possibilities.

"For this area, it is. It is also protected from misuse, for we have dug wells deep into the ground and are able to transport in food and supplies." I stopped at the large pool, let go of her hand. "Today, it belongs to us."

"Us?" she wondered, wandering about, taking it all in.

She was so lovely in her curiosity. She wasn't fearful of Trion, of me, and for that I was thankful.

"You and me. No one will enter Mirana but us. It is ours until the suns rise tomorrow."

"Suns? Earth only has one." Tilting her chin back, she looked up at the sky. "I don't see them."

"It would hurt your eyes if you did. That is why it is so warm, why Mirana is such a treat, for it is cool within. We have two moons, as well. Tonight, when the stars are thick, you will see them." I held out my hand.

"Come, it is time to bathe."

After the exam, I had been patient and relaxed. No longer. She was at the pool where we could bathe and swim together, an outdoor rarity on Trion. Alone. That meant she would be naked, wet and just for me.

She came around the pool and took my hand. Hers was so

small, so delicate I worried my needs would be too much for her. The lusty way she came on the probe made me think she was much stronger than I originally assumed, and for that I was thankful. By dawn, I would have her so many different ways, none of them tame or meant to ease her into the life as my mate, for I would not hold back this night. I would not allow her to be tame; I wanted her wild and uninhibited. I hoped she was strong, mentally as well as physically. Being mate to a councilor would not be easy either, as there would be many demands on our time. Moments like this, when we were truly alone, would be few and far between.

But not now. Not today. Today she was all mine and mine alone. No one to hear. No one to see.

I pushed the robe off her shoulders and it slid down her body to the verdant ground. I sucked in a breath at the sight of her, her skin glowing with the soft natural light. The sight of the disks dangling from the chain made me hard. Too hard for the confines of my pants, so I stripped quickly.

Her eyes flared wide at seeing me bare. I didn't know how Earth males were formed, but Trions were large, over a head taller than Natalie. While she was fair of hair and skin, I was olive toned, my skin tanned by the sun. My dark hair was not just on my head and face, but a smattering spread across my chest and down to my navel, then lower to the thatch at the base of my erect cock.

I wasn't soft or very attractive, my body well muscled and hard. My cock was more a club than member and I worried for a brief moment Natalie would find me unappealing. When her cheeks flushed and her nipples hardened before my eyes, I exhaled the breath I hadn't realized I'd been holding. Since when had I ever cared what someone thought?

Since I'd taken a mate.

"Are all Trion males like you?" she asked, staring at my cock, which made it pulse involuntarily.

"Like me how?"

"Big. Um… huge."

I looked down at myself curiously. I looked like a typical Trion warrior.

"What are males like on Earth?" I asked, then waved my hand in the air. "Never mind. I don't want to know about any other cocks you've seen… or—"

At the direction of my thoughts I saw red. No one should touch Natalie but me.

She smiled at me, stepped closer, put her hand on my chest. "I am not a virgin."

I growled then. I couldn't help it.

"I can't change my past. But know this," she added, moving her hand down my belly, then lower still, to grip me. My hips bucked into her hold. "He was nothing like this. He had a pencil dick in comparison and didn't know how to use it."

She tilted her head back and looked at me, met my eyes with her pale ones.

In this moment, I was at her mercy. Completely, totally. I could start wars with her hand around my cock. If I had any brain function left, I would ask her what a pencil dick was.

"You do know how to use it, don't you?" she murmured, sliding her hand up to swipe the drop of pre-cum from the tip.

No, she was not tame at all.

"Earth female, you are too tempting. I was going to bathe you first, ease you into the hard fucking I will give you, for you are new to Trion ways, but not now."

* * *

NATALIE

. . .

45

ONE MINUTE I was standing before Roark, my hand boldly on his cock, the next I was on my back staring up at the thick foliage of the oasis. His hands stroked from my shoulders to my breasts, cupping and playing with them, brushing his thumbs over the nipples, bumping the small rings.

I wasn't sure if it was Roark that made them so sensitive or if it was the rings. I didn't care, just arched my back into his palms wanting more. As soon as I did so, he moved his hands lower, over my ribs, my belly, my hips and then between. Not to touch my pussy. No, Roark seemed to be hell-bent on making me suffer through exquisite pleasure. Pushing my thighs apart, he settled between them, lowering himself so his head hovered right above my core. Coming up on my elbows, I stared down my body at him. Dark hair, serious gaze, well-placed hands.

"I can smell your arousal. Sweet and tangy. I can see it slip from you. It's time to taste."

When he lowered his head and I felt his tongue slide up the length of me, I cried out and gripped his hair.

"Oh my god."

My head fell back and I closed my eyes, giving myself over to his wicked mouth. He flicked, he swirled, he slid, he sucked. Laved. Kissed. Curtis had attempted it once, but had given up quickly, wanting his turn, the selfish little shit. I never asked for oral after that, knowing it wasn't his thing. But Roark, holy hell, eating me out was definitely his thing. His tongue, his mouth, were so damn skilled that I went from zero to sixty faster than ever in my life. Was it because I was bare there or that he had a beard, or both? When he slipped a finger into me and magically curled it, I came.

My body shuddered and I closed my thighs around his head, holding him right where he was.

"That's... oh shit, you found my G-spot." I crooned when

he prolonged the pleasure with a little twist or nudge somewhere that had eluded everyone. Until now.

Sweat bloomed on my skin. Every nerve ending came alive. I could feel the soft robe beneath my back, the muscles of his shoulders against my thighs, his hand on my hip holding me down, the weight of the chain on my belly, the little rings through my nipples.

Roark sat back on his heels, used the back of his hand to wipe his mouth, yet his beard still glistened. Oh my, that was from me. I'd never been so wet before, so eager. His cock jutted up and toward me and I licked my lips. I wanted it. Wanted to taste him, to feel him against my tongue.

Coming up quickly, I tucked my legs beneath me and lowered my head. With my hands on his thighs, the soft hair there silky and springy against my palms, I leaned down and licked the broad crown of his massive cock. A pearly drop of fluid seeped from the narrow slit and slid down. Eagerly, I licked it up, tasting him for the first time.

He hissed out a breath and his hips jerked. Glancing up at him through my lashes, I saw his jaw clenched tight, his eyes narrowed and filled with lust, his hands were tight in fists and his belly was taut. Every line of his body was tense as if waiting for my tongue to touch again. Was he even breathing?

I felt powerful in that moment. Just a simple flick of my tongue and I'd rendered him... what? When I circled my tongue around the ridge of the head, he growled. I felt it even in my palms on his thighs. I didn't wait then, only took him in my mouth, my lips opening wide to accommodate all of him.

Wow, he was big. I wouldn't be able to fit all of him in my mouth. I'd have to be a porn star to take that monster, and down my throat? Not a chance. But he tasted good, salty and pungent, and his scent was all male. I couldn't resist his balls, the heavy weight of them in my palm attested to his virility. That was all for me? No wonder I had to be tested. I wasn't sure if it was going to fit.

All this flitted through my mind as I sucked on him, but a hand tangled in my hair, gripped tightly and pulled me back.

"I am the one in control, mate," Roark said. His eyes were black, his jaw tight. The hand in my hair was not gentle, but I loved his show of strength, of his power over me.

With a gentle tug on my hair, I went onto my back. He looked down at me as he pushed one leg wide, dropped his hand beside my head to hold himself up, found my entrance and thrust into me.

I gasped and arched at the sudden fullness. With his hand still in place, forcing me to hold his gaze, I could see he was right there with me. Releasing his grip, he slid it down my body, over my breast, flicked the ring.

His hips shifted, making me forget all about his nipple play. He was big and I was not. It was a tight fit, but he'd prepared me. I was soft and swollen, wet and eager and he somehow knew I could handle him, that I didn't want him to ease in. I didn't want gentle.

Gripping his sides, I held on as he pulled back, then plunged deep again. My breasts swayed, the chain heavy and pulling.

He opened his eyes and looked at me, watched as he took me.

"This is going to be fast, Natalie. Your hot mouth around my cock ruined my control. *Fark.*" He didn't seem too pleased with that.

I liked seeing him get lost in his baser needs, his hips pumping in a rhythm that was far from controlled. His skin became slick beneath my palms, his breaths ragged.

He'd made me come once, but I was ready again. The places inside, that he'd awakened with his finger, liked the friction caused by his cock. I couldn't help but clench down on him, hoping to hold him within.

He hissed at the squeeze and when he went deep, I did it again. And again until I couldn't take it anymore.

"I'm… I'm going to come. Roark, I've never… it's—"

"Come. Come now and I will follow you over."

I did what he commanded and came, my back arching, my knees coming up and squeezing his hips. I milked his cock, my inner walls rippling around him, coating him with my arousal that never seemed to stop.

Hooking a hand behind my knee, he lifted and adjusted the angle, drove home and stiffened above me. His face looked pained, his face reddening, the muscles in his neck taut. A groan ripped from his throat as I felt his cock pulse, the seed hot as it coated me. Marked me.

He pulled out and sat back, his cock still just as hard, just as angry red, but now glistened in my wetness and his seed.

"You're—"

"Not done," he replied, his eyes were passion-filled and looking directly at me, as if I was prey and he was about to pounce. Gripping my hip, he flipped me onto my belly, tugged back so I came up on my knees.

Before I could look over my shoulder, a hand came down on my bottom with a loud crack.

"Roark!" I cried, not in anger, but surprise.

Glancing at him, he grinned, although it was feral. "That's for being too hot. Too sexy. Too damn perfect for my cock. Look at you."

He kept his hand on my hip, securing me in place, although I had no intention of going anywhere.

"I love seeing my chain dangle from your breasts, my handprint pink on your ass, your pussy all swollen and well used, my seed dripping from it."

He spanked me again. "I told you I was the one in control."

He shifted, aligning himself up with me again, then pushed in. His passage this time was eased by his copious seed.

"More," he said, his voice deep. "You will give me everything."

I closed my eyes, reveled in the hot feel of him, the stretch, the fullness. "More," I repeated, wiggling my hips, then pushing back against him.

That afforded me another swat to the butt, but this time I just tensed, then savored the feel of the sting as it morphed into heat.

It was too much. He was too much. Reaching between my legs, I found my clit and began to rub it. I just needed that little bit, and while I had every confidence in Roark to make me come on his own, I was greedy. He said as much.

"So needy for your pleasure. You can't wait, can you?"

He continued to fuck me, his need hadn't waned even after coming once already. In fact, he thrust his hips with more vigor now. I was with him every step of the way and I wanted that third orgasm.

Now.

Rubbing and circling my clit, I came, the feel of his cock my undoing. *He* was my undoing.

Perhaps it was how I milked him once again, perhaps he got off on spanking my ass and seeing it turn red. Perhaps he was just horny, but he came directly after me.

As soon as he released my hip, I slumped down on the robe, wilted. Done. Glancing over my shoulder at him, I saw how he looked at my pussy, put his fingers there and collected the seed that had begun to slip out and work it back into me.

"Mine," he said again, taking hold of the chain and gently

tugging. I hissed at the pleasurable pain. "You carry my chain. Your scent is mixed with mine now. You're coated and marked by my seed. No one will ever take you from me. You're my mate now, Natalie. My life. You're mine."

He continued to tug as if waiting for something. I nodded and whispered, "Yes." Only then did he let the warmed chain drop to my damp skin.

He lay down beside me and gathered me into his arms. I went willingly, never so content in my life. I loved everything about this man, his gruff manner, his dirty talk, the way he touched me. But most of all, I loved knowing I mattered to him. After years of cold, uninterested parents, and a luke-warm relationship with my fiancé, feeling cherished and wanted, adored…it was heaven.

He wrapped his arms around me and stroked my back with gentle hands. I felt like I was being petted, treasured, and I was, in that moment, eternally grateful to the Inter-stellar Brides Program. They'd promised me a perfect match. And, lying here in his arms, I couldn't argue with their process. Roark was mine. And I was never going back to the empty life I'd had before.

This was my home now. Roark, with his wild fucking and remarkable tenderness. *He* was my home. And soon, I would no doubt be pregnant with our first child. I was going to have a mate who loved me, who adored me, who fucked me like a wild man, and a baby, too. A baby, to hug and kiss and cuddle.

My heart hurt, it was so full of hope and dreams and contentment.

I smiled, my head nestled against his chest and wrapped my arms around him. "You're mine, too, Roark."

He squeezed me, his hand drifting from the curve of my bottom to my shoulder. I had a suspicion that Trion mates didn't say that to their *masters*, but I felt it, felt that I was as much his as he was mine. And I told him so, not afraid of him or his more demanding ways. We'd been matched, the testing complete. He tugged on the chain between my nipples because he knew I liked it, even without asking. He knew I liked his hand spanking my bottom.

After a moment, he responded. "Yes, mate. I am yours."

"Only mine."

I would not travel across the universe for a mate to seek comfort in another. I could have stayed on Earth and been satisfied with Curtis.

"I will have no other, Natalie. You are mine."

Exactly.

I fell asleep happy, smiling and sated, the gentle stroking of his fingers a balm to my bruised soul. This was heaven, all right. I'd travelled across the galaxy to find heaven…and fall in love.

oark

"WAKE UP, *gara*. I haven't worn you out that much, hmm?" I lay beside Natalie and was propped up on my elbow, gazing at her. She was beautiful in her sleep, especially since I knew the reason for her weariness. *I'd* done this to her. I'd worn her out with too many orgasms. Too much fucking.

I'd never gone twice like that before, but when I'd come the first time, my cock just wasn't done. It didn't soften, not even a little bit, not even after filling her to the brim with seed. My cock wanted more and so I'd flipped her over and had her again.

I nuzzled my nose down her long neck, breathing in her personal scent and the musky aroma of fucking. She murmured and tilted her head for me to continue, but didn't awaken.

"How have you done it?" I murmured aloud, speaking to Natalie, but more to the universe at large. The family medallions affixed to the chain rested on her smooth belly. Seeing them on her was powerful, intense even. I never imagined I would be this possessive, this protective of a female, an alien Earth female, who I'd just met.

The match was incredible. I felt a connection with her that went so much deeper than slaking my physical needs in her body. I needed *her*. Needed something that only she could give me, and fucking? That was how I could get inside her and be a part of her. I needed to be part of her.

"You are mine, Natalie Montgomery from Earth. I didn't really want a mate, but—"

Her eyes came open then. Of course, right then.

"You didn't?" she asked, blinking once, then again, a worried look coming over her face.

I stroked my hand over her cheek. "You didn't let me finish. I didn't really want a mate. My mother felt it was time to continue the line."

Her pert nose crinkled. "Your mother? How can you speak about your mother when we are naked?"

I couldn't help but smile. "I will finish this, then speak of her no more this day. I agreed to a mate, for it was time, and if the brides program could find the perfect female for me, then it was… efficient."

She laughed and rolled her eyes. "Efficient?"

Running a hand over her hair, I collected it into my palm, closed my fingers, then tugged, tilting her head toward me. Her eyes opened wide at the dominant action.

"Do not roll your eyes at me, mate. Any other time and you would be over my lap." I paused, let that sink in. "To answer your question, yes, efficient. I needed a female to breed and I received one via transport. You. But I didn't expect to find a mate for my cock, my heart. My soul."

Her eyes went from surprised to gentle.

"You… you feel it, too? I was afraid to say anything. It's so soon," she whispered.

I released her hair and moved over her, pressing some of my weight into her, feeling every soft inch. Her hard, pebbled nipples pressed against my chest. I felt the curved rings, the line of chain, the medallions.

"I feel it. The intense pleasure being inside you. The need to join together. I want to crawl up inside you and never leave."

She laughed and I loved seeing the way her whole face softened and came alive. "I don't think you'll fit." Lifting her hand, she stroked down my cheek, feeling my beard. "Your cock will do."

"And my seed."

Her cheeks flushed. "You're so adamant about your seed being in me."

I nodded gravely. "I am. It shows you are mine, marked. It shows you have pleased me and that I have pleased you in return. Soon, you will be round with my child. For now, it shows that I *can* be deep inside you, that that's where I belong."

I pushed up to sitting, reached for the necklace about my neck, took it off and held it up for her to see.

"This disk has my symbol on it." I gripped the round medallion that dangled from the chain. It wasn't heavy, but it was dense. The two swords crossed pressed into the precious metal was my personal symbol. "The ones on your chain indicate you are mine through my family. No one will doubt my claim on you with them. But this—" I slipped the disk from the necklace's chain, tossed it up in the air, let it land in my palm, then handed it to her. She studied it as I continued. "—is my own medallion and with it affixed to your chain, will show that you are mine because I chose to give this to

55

you. As you are not from Trion, you do not understand this significance. It is more than a simple disk, it is my life."

It was the key to the southern continent's subterranean vault. The people of Trion chose to live a simpler life, but that did not mean we were a primitive race. Our technology and weapons were in league with the other races of the Coalition. The vault held wealth and weaponry, knowledge and a record of the ancient bloodlines. With the key, I gave Natalie the most precious gift I could give her. I made her a member of my family, a powerful member, as only myself, my father and my sister had access to the vault. The key required my DNA to activate, but I wanted Natalie to have it. Seeing the symbol of my devotion on her body made my cock hard and my heart ache.

With my power came responsibility, but also danger. Those who would want to overthrow the government—me— would want the secrets that were held within. Sharing it with Natalie meant I found her my equal, not just my bed partner. She didn't understand this yet and no explanations would clarify this for her. Over time, she'd learn she carried the hope and trust of the entire southern continent between her breasts, affixed to the most intimate places on her body.

"Sit up, please." I offered her my hand and tugged her to sitting, the chain dangling from her gorgeous breasts swayed. "You are beautiful," I murmured.

I took the medallion from her fingers. "I was going to wait, Natalie, the thirty days. To let you decide in your own time, or at least in the time the brides program allows, to make your choice. But I don't want to wait. I know that you belong to me. I want forever, Natalie. I'll wait if you demand it, but I want you now. I know you belong to me. Say yes."

She licked her lips, studied me, looked down at her transformation from Earth female to Trion mate. *My* mate. The chain, the medallions, the shaved pussy, the seed slipping from her. It was an outward indicator that she belonged to me. But on the inside, she had yet to make a choice. I was pushing her, I knew, but I couldn't help it. I couldn't wait. The need made it impossible.

"Do you wish to be mine and mine alone? Can I claim you now?"

Tears filled her eyes, then slid down her cheeks.

"*Fark*," I swore, then stroked my fingers over her cheek. "No, it's all right. You can take the time to—"

"No. I mean yes. These are tears of happiness. Yes, I want you to claim me now. I don't need thirty days to decide."

She smiled brilliantly then and something bright filled my chest, made me grin at her in return. Love. It had to be. It was radiant and wonderful and she'd given it to me. A precious gift. And so I gave her my medallion in return. Taking the chain, I carefully affixed my personal medallion to it, the small, automated hook activated by my DNA. No one could remove the disk, nor activate it. Only those with my family's DNA could do so.

Releasing the small gold medallion, I watched as the chain swayed, now adorned with three disks. "The marks within the medallions represent me, my family line and my place as councilor. They proclaim for one and all that you are mine, and that I will kill to protect you."

And the extra medallion, no larger than the nail on my smallest finger, dangled low, at the center, nearly over her womb, and, like her womb would carry my child, the gold carried the future, the power and wealth accumulated over many generations of my family.

She lifted her head and looked to me. "My nipples are sensitive. They… they tingle and it's constant. Arousing."

I glanced down at my cock, which was thick, long and pointing straight at her. "Yes, I know what you mean."

I came over her so she had no choice but to lower onto

her back. Settling on my forearms above her, I pressed her into the soft ground so she felt all of me, from thigh to shoulder. Between our bellies, I could feel the chain, the medallions. I knew the secrets would be safe with her, and that she would be safe with me. Nothing would happen to her. I would protect her with my life.

Lowering my head, I kissed her. It was the first time. When her soft lips brushed mine, I had to wonder how I'd skipped something so intimate until now. How had I not put my mouth on hers? I'd put it on her pussy, but this seemed more personal. Her mouth opened readily for mine and my tongue found hers. She gasped at the decadence of something so simple and my cock pulsed.

I could kiss her until the two moons rose and I'd be content, but my cock had other ideas. She'd consented to the claiming and I could think of nothing else.

I lifted my head so our breaths still mingled, that I could look into her pale eyes. My hips shifted so I settled into the cradle of her own, my cock nestled at her slippery entrance. It was hot and wet, all but inviting me in. "Do you accept me, Natalie Montgomery of Earth, as your mate? Do you accept my claim on you, that I am your master?"

"Yes." She arched her back, angled her hips into me so that my cock slipped in an inch. "Yes, claim me. I want it. I want you. *Master.*"

My eyes fell closed then, awash with the sensations of this woman calling me master. The feeling was heady, the one word so weighty with responsibility. I was responsible for every facet of Natalie. Her happiness, her wellbeing, her health, her safety. Everything.

And when I slid into her, slowly this time, I accepted it.

"Mine," I growled as I kept my gaze fixed on hers. She was so hot, so wet that I moved so smoothly up into her. She didn't close her eyes, didn't look away as I took her as gently as I possibly could, letting her feel every inch of me. We weren't lost in the fiery haze of passion, we were lost in tenderness, in each other.

"Mine," she whispered, lifting her hips to take me deeper, then deeper still.

We were one. When she came with soft shudders and rippling walls of her pussy, I went with her.

"Natalie," I groaned, giving over to her in every way.

We remained in the oasis for long hours, talking and learning each other. I bathed her in the warm water of the small pond and fed her fresh fruit transported in from the north, tasting the ripe berry juice on her lips.

I took her again, reveled in her eager welcome, her soft sighs and cries of pleasure. And when I knew my seed filled her, my medallions marked her as mine, and the soft glow on her face would shout to one and all her contentment with her mate, I took her back to civilization, eager to show her our home in the capital city of Xalia.

I pulled a long, cream-colored dress from the supplies I'd left here in preparation and draped the soft fabric over her naked form. The piercings in her nipples were clearly visible through the fabric and my chest swelled with pride at the vision she presented. Her soft, golden hair hung loose and wild around her shoulders. Her fair skin practically glowed above the neckline of the gown, and her eyes, those eyes, looked at me with complete trust and devotion. I dared to believe that, perhaps, my mate had grown to love me in such a short time.

Pulling her along, I strode from the oasis with her by my side. A contingent of my personal guards, Byran among them, stood at attention on all sides of the oasis, ensuring both our privacy and safety.

"Councilor." Byran bowed slightly, a frown on his brow. "I did not wish to disturb you, but there have been reports of

Drovers on the fringe of the territory. We believe they are massing for an attack."

Natalie stiffened and stepped closer, pressing herself to my side, instinctively trusting me to protect and shelter her. Her trust made my heart ache, even as the Drover threat made my blood rage. The Drovers had not dared attack an outpost in years, instead attacking traveling caravans or small parties, like the raiders and pirates they were. Scum.

"Gather the men. We must eliminate this threat before we can go home. We will not leave the outpost unprotected."

"Yes, sir." Byran motioned to half a dozen of my men who ran after him to reach the others, warriors stationed strategically around the outpost. I was at Outpost Two, as were three tribal chiefs from my territory. All told, we had a force of no more than two hundred men. I prayed it would be enough.

I looked down at my mate as another seven of my most trusted warriors surrounded us. "Don't worry, mate. The Drovers cannot reach you here."

"What are Drovers?" Her eyes had grown dark with worry and I longed to replace the expression with the one she'd had earlier. Longing. Trust. Love. Those were the only emotions I wanted to see in those beautiful pale eyes.

A guard handed me my sword and an ion blaster. Forced to release my mate long enough to strap the weapons securely to my waist, I missed her warmth instantly. "Come, mate. I will explain all in due time. For now, I will take you to the transport center. You will be safe there, with the doctor, while I deal with these invaders."

We'd taken two steps when the first explosions roared through camp, their blasts loud as a desert sandstorm. But there was no sand...only fire.

CHAPTER 7

*N*atalie

I FOLLOWED Roark from the oasis, his large hand around mine was firm, but warm and gentle. My insides were so scrambled I couldn't process all the emotion running through my body. The connection between us was instant, and so powerful that I couldn't even look at him now without my heart racing. He'd been dominant and demanding, fucking me like a caveman, even tugging on my hair. But then he turned into a gentle giant and nearly ripped my heart into pieces with his tenderness.

He was everything I'd ever dreamed of in bed. I had high hopes that he'd be everything I dreamed of out of it as well.

We emerged from the oasis and I knew from the heat in my cheeks that I blushed as his soldiers stood at attention. They each inspected me with open curiosity, but I did my best to ignore them. I would not behave in any way to bring dishonor to my mate, so I held my head high, thrust my chest forward proudly, the chain and medallions, the mark of Roark's family, clearly visible through the thin fabric of my dress. The weight tugged at my nipples constantly, teasing me with sensation and leaving my in a never-ending state of arousal.

Not that I minded. I had a feeling all it would take was one look from me and I'd be on my hands and knees with my wild lover filling me from behind any time I wanted.

Dozens of tents sprawled in the middle of the desert landscape as if they'd popped into existence from nothing. They clumped around the center tent, the largest where—Roark had pointed out—the transport station was hidden. Beyond the edges of the outpost I saw nothing but sand for miles in every direction with an occasional dark smudge of what I assumed was a hearty bush or rock. On my right, just beyond the edge of camp, a rock formation rose from the middle of the desert like sentinels watching over the outpost. A slight breeze kept me from feeling miserable in the heat, a trail of sand clearly visible where the wind pushed the small grains around the edges of the rocks.

A wind block, then? Did the wind usually come from that direction? And what direction was it? I had no idea.

The world was alien and strange, but oddly beautiful. I felt like I'd stepped into the pages of a fairy-tale adventure. *Arabian Nights*. I glanced up at the sky, noting that their large sun was fully overhead, the soft yellow glow warm and welcome on my bare arms. But on the horizon, newly rising, a dark red sun climbed in the sky and I wondered what they called it. I'd never seen a red sun before, and I wondered if it would feel hot when it blazed its brightest overhead. Roark had said there were two moons as well, but he'd kept me too busy to notice them.

"Councilor." One of his men bowed slightly. He was tall and dark, as they all were, and had a furrowed brow. He was younger than Roark by perhaps a decade. "I did not wish to disturb you, but there have been reports of Drovers on the fringe of the territory. We believe they are massing for an attack."

I stepped closer to Roark. Their talk of an attack made me nervous, but Roark's huge bulk made me feel safe. As did the presence of a dozen more equally massive and well-armed males. Each of them was at least six foot six with a wicked-looking sword on one hip and some kind of silver, space gun on the other. I had no idea what a Drover was, nor did I care. Not right now. I only worried that Roark might be injured while fighting them.

My mate looked down at me as his men surrounded us in a cocoon of protection. "Don't worry, mate. The Drovers cannot reach you here." He looked calm and completely in control. I believed him, the tension in my body retreating to a manageable level. This was his world, not mine. I would have to trust him. But that didn't mean I would remain ignorant of the threats around us.

"What are Drovers?"

"Come, mate." He tugged on my hand. "I will explain everything in due time. For now, I will take you to the transport center. You will be safe there, with the doctor, while I deal with these invaders."

Roark's command spurred my feet into action. He'd given me soft sandals that sank into the white sand as I walked. It was warm underfoot, but not scorching hot. I took two steps when a bomb went off.

Before I knew what happened, I was on the ground, Roark's massive frame covering me.

A wall of fire shot out overhead but disappeared in the blink of an eye. I heard screams and men shouting on the edge of camp, near the tall rocks.

I could barely breathe, and was about to protest Roark's heavy bulk when he lifted off me.

"Are you injured?" He rolled onto his side, his back to the shouts, protecting me with his body as his eyes drifted over me from head to toe. Fierce, intense, concerned. Gone was the gentle lover.

"I'm okay."

"What is O-K? Letters? You speak to me in letters?" His gaze intensified and he lifted his chin, never taking his eyes from me. "Doctor!"

His roar hurt my ears but I lifted my hand to his cheek to soothe him. Obviously, the translator thing implanted behind our ears didn't translate American slang. "I'm fine, Roark. I'm not hurt. Just shaken up a bit."

He lowered his head to mine for a quick kiss as the doctor he'd summoned appeared, her sandals a few inches from my head on the sand. "Councilor?" she asked.

Roark rose to his feet, pulling me with him. The chain swung beneath my loose dress. "Take my mate to the transport station and protect her with your life."

"Roark, no..." I didn't want the woman killing herself to protect me. We were in this together now, the two of us. It was Roark and me against the world, against the Drovers. "Give me one of those gun things. I can fight."

His warriors surrounded us in a loose circle, swords in one hand and guns in the other. He shook his head. "No, mate. You will go with the doctor."

"What? Why? Where are you going?"

He turned, his scowl fierce and frightening. I would not want to be one of those Drovers right now. "I must make sure my parents transported back to Xalia. If not, I need to ensure they are protected. Once they are secure, I will kill the Drovers."

So, parents. Drovers. Then me. Okay. Fine. I could deal. I nodded. "Make sure you come back to me."

"I give you my word, Natalie. I will come to you immediately once the battle is over. But first I must ensure my parents left yesterday, as planned." Roark placed a small dagger in my hand, pressing the handle tightly to my palm until I wrapped shaking fingers around the hilt. It was small, not much longer than my fingers, and the blade was a bright, brilliant gold. "Take this. Keep it with you at all times."

I nod as the doctor tugged on my arm and I took a step in her direction. I had a bad feeling about this. Roark turned from me and ordered two of his men to accompany us to the transport station. The two warriors grabbed each of us by the arm and began to run as a second explosion sounded.

I turned back to watch my mate bellow orders into the chaos. He was a mountain among his men, fierce and strong, and completely focused on finding his parents and securing the camp. He turned, scanning the site with a predator's gaze. That scrutiny flitted over me, through me, past me, is if I were already forgotten.

"Don't be a baby," I scolded myself as I ran with the doctor. She was half a head taller than me, and strong. I was running, but she dragged me about every third step because I couldn't keep up with her in the sand. She may have been used to running on a beach, but I wasn't. The transport station wasn't far, but I was winded and scared by the time the doctor and I ducked under the tent flap. The two warriors with us stood at the entrance, weapons out and ready. The noises outside the tent were nothing like when I first arrived. Calmness ensued then. Now, without even being able to see, I knew something was wrong. Fear, panic, death could be heard through the thin walls.

The doctor closed the flap and wrapped me in a quick

hug, girl to girl, and I really needed it. "Tell me everything's going to be fine, even if you have to lie."

The doctor pulled back and smiled. "Everything's going to be fine. And I'm not lying. Councilor Roark wouldn't have sent you here otherwise." She released me, pointed to the transport platform. "But I'm also cautious."

"What do you mean?"

She pointed. "Get up there. I'm going to get the transport codes ready, just in case."

"Just in case?" I knew what she was saying, but I didn't want to hear it. I didn't want to leave Roark behind.

"Your mate asked me to protect you and this is what I'm doing." She was a doctor and seemed to remain cool under pressure, but I could see her eyes were slightly wild, her hands quick. "This is the only way out of here with the Drovers everywhere."

"Where are you going to send me?"

"It takes a couple minutes to power up, then a few more to enter new coordinates. Right now, this thing is still set to Earth." She waved at me again, but didn't look up from what she was doing at the transport controls. I felt like I was on a *Star Trek* episode waiting to say, *"Beam me up, Scotty."*

I stood and wiped the sand off my skin. I was covered, the fine grains coating my arms and chest and clinging like glitter to the soft fabric of my dress. It fell, spreading in a random mess all over the transport pad.

"Hurry. Hurry." The doctor muttered under her breath and I stopped with my hands on my thighs, rubbing at the sand. A loud clattering of metal, of sword striking sword, sounded from the entrance of the tent. The doctor cursed in her native tongue and I jumped, screaming as one of our guards flew backward through the entrance, a knife sticking out of his left eye socket.

"Go! Now!" Our remaining guard roared the order as he

backed into the entrance. He fought three men that I could see. These Drovers were smaller than he, but fast and vicious. They were covered, head to toe in a dark brown robe and scarves that reminded me of desert nomads I'd seen on *National Geographic*. Their smaller swords flashing through the air so quickly I had trouble tracking the battle with my eyes.

"No!" I screamed. "What about Roark? Where's Roark?"

The doctor shook her head, shouting even as she worked the controls. "He's dead. I'm sorry. If they're here, he's already dead. I have to get you away from here."

"Dead? No!"

No. He couldn't be dead.

No. No. No.

The doctor yelled at me but I could no longer hear her. The floor vibrated beneath my feet. A bright blue light erupted from previously unseen lines. The brightness made me squint in pain as it formed a strange grid pattern on the transport pad. I tried to move off the pad, but I was trapped by the energy rising to choke me in a cloud of power and I could not breathe. The guard I'd barely met fell to his knees and one Drover slit his throat as another plunged a dagger into his side. I tried to reach out to them, to scream, but I couldn't do anything. I could only watch and do nothing.

Behind the doctor, the third Drover raced to her and plunged a dagger into her back. She screamed, I saw her mouth open as she sank to her knees, but I heard nothing now, nothing but the hum of the transport. One Drover plunged his knife into our guard's chest, over and over as I stood, frozen, watching with growing horror as the other attacker rushed toward me.

He lunged through the bright blue light, his gnarled and calloused hand grasping at me.

His fist tightened in my dress, tugging me mercilessly,

relentlessly forward. I braced my feet and struck his arm with the dagger I still held. The gold blade struck his arm. Blood splattered on my dress, but he did not release me. Terrified, I pulled away from him with every ounce of strength I possessed. I felt the seam of my dress pop along my back as the dress ripped in two. The Drover fell back with a yell when the garment fell away from me, the seam in back exploding with a tearing sound that rattled my teeth.

Naked but for my sandals and the chains hanging from my breasts, I screamed at him, enraged that he'd killed the doctor, stabbed her in the back. Cold blooded. They'd also taken my mate from me. *This* was to be my fate on this stupid planet. The man I'd just begun to love, who had officially claimed me, was dead?

The hum surrounding me changed to a roar so loud I feared my skull would explode. I could not even scream as everything went black.

CHAPTER 8

R *oark*

THE CHAINS around my wrists had worn through flesh to
bone and a fever raged in my blood. My restraints were
affixed to a heavy wooden post that ran the length of the
Drovers' tent. I'd been beaten and starved, tortured for four
long days, and still the Drovers had not revealed the reason
for their attack, nor what they wanted from me.

I was surprised I still lived. The Drovers were not known
for taking prisoners. Nor for torture. They preferred to
strike and run. To kill indiscriminately, leaving no survivors.
Ransom, perhaps? I heard of no other prisoners, saw none. I
had to assume I'd been the only one caught. But why? Why
was I still alive?

Something had changed, something fundamental to the
future of my people. If the Drovers were employing new
tactics, I needed to figure out why. I couldn't do it strung up
like meat in this tent. I remembered searching for my

parents, learning that they had transported as I'd wished. They were safe at home in Xalia.

Trying to clear the sand from my dry eyes, I blinked slowly, my entire body alive with pain.

And through it all, my only thoughts were of Natalie. My Natalie. My mate.

She had escaped their clutches. Of this I was certain. For if they had her, they would have used her against me, brought her here and tortured her before my eyes. They would have used her to break me. And, gods help me, they would have succeeded. I'd never tasted such heaven as I had in her arms. I would do anything to protect her, anything at all.

I had to get away, to find her. She was alone on Trion. She knew no one. *Fark*, she'd only been on the planet for a few days. The distance between us was more painful than the punishment the Drovers were inflicting on my body. She was saving me by just being in my thoughts. She was my motivation, my drive to remain alive. I promised her I wouldn't leave her alone, that I'd protect her, and I was failing her with every minute that passed, every beat of my heart.

I couldn't remain like this, chained. I had to escape. As I fumed, our suns set and the world became dark. There were no lights in the tent, the faint light of dusk barely penetrating the thick walls of the tent. My eyes adjusted to the darkness and I looked up as the tent flapped opened and a single Drover entered. They had arrived in groups the first day, perhaps concerned I would fight them. Now, they were confident, cocky that they'd tamped my spirit and were slowly crushing my body.

They were wrong. I was invigorated by their laziness. My weakened muscles now pumped with adrenaline. My hands clenched into fists in readiness.

The Drover never met my eye, only held his ion blaster in

one hand and used a key to undo the chain from my wrist restraints. His stench filled my nostrils, acrid and bitter. Sweat and bitter oils made my nose burn. These bastards were barely above animals, would work for anyone who had coin. I wouldn't fight him here, not in the tent. I had to see how many others there were. I knew the basic layout of their compound from the other times they took me to a different tent to beat me. The Drovers who held me were not part of a large group, only a few tents made up the nomadic camp.

A push at my shoulder blades had me stumbling out into the fresh air. I looked about, although I could only see as far as the glow lanterns that hung from wooden stakes. All was quiet except for the snuffling sounds of their *nox*, the large animals they used as transport. The giant beasts were penned somewhere nearby. I didn't like the quiet as it was deceiving. The Drovers weren't ones to speak or socialize unnecessarily, and while there were no sounds coming from the various tents, I knew more enemies lurked than the one nudging me along.

The sand was still warm beneath my bare feet. I took a step, then another, ensuring no one was about, maintaining awareness of my surroundings. I could fight this one Drover easily enough, I just had to do it quietly.

Before we made it around the tent, I spun about, my elbow bumping into his wrist, shifting the ion pistol away from me. Stepping in close, his arm was along my hip, blocking the pistol. If he fired, it would be heard across the compound. I had to move quickly. Lightning fast, I lifted my arms over his head, the restraints hooked behind his robed neck. Because he was small, as all Drovers were, I loomed over him. Taking my right hand, I circled down and under my left to wrap the restraints about his neck. Punching upward toward the black sky, I broke his trachea, silencing any call he had for help. I winced at the pain in my wrenched

71

shoulder, but pushed through. With both hands on the side of his head, I grabbed hold and twisted back, breaking his neck.

I had to unwind my arms to allow him to fall to the sand. Dead. Squatting down, I grabbed his ion pistol and scanned the area. My right knee screamed in protest. I breathed through my mouth, trying to keep as quiet as possible through the sharp stab of pain. Still no one.

A quick search of his body and I had the keys to my restraints. As quickly as I could, I unlocked my wrists and tossed the hated leather and buckles away from me, out into the desert to be swallowed by the ever-moving sand.

Keeping away from the lantern light, I followed the occasional sound of the *nox* and knew they were my means for escape. I found the temporary pen easily, went to the farthest animal and found the bucket on the ground filled with water. I didn't care that a *nox* had drunk from it first. I'd barely been given any water during my captivity. Dropping to my good knee, I scooped the water into my palm, gulped it down. Only when I'd had my fill did I rise and grab the animal's lead. Lifting the rope that formed the edge of the pen, I led the *nox* away. When I was far enough from the camp that a grumble or protest from the beast would not alert my enemies, I struggled up onto the beast's back.

Slumping forward, I breathed through the pain and assessed my injuries. A bad knee, perhaps a torn tendon. A broken finger. Concussion. Multiple broken ribs. Lacerations on my thighs from their knives and on my back from the lash. And I was burning with fever, from Drover poison or infection, I could not say. Colors pulsed and danced before my eyes against the blackness of the desert night as the beast lurched between my legs. I dug my heels into the animal's hairy flanks and fought to remain conscious as the gentle giant plodded into the desert.

I was definitely in need of food and dehydrated. I needed to get to Outpost Two and the transport station before I passed out, fell to the sand and the *nox* wandered off. It was the only way back home, to help. To find Natalie.

* * *

NATALIE, Earth, November

I SAT on the bathroom floor of my hotel room and hugged the toilet. Nausea had woken me from a fitful sleep an hour ago. Even though I'd thrown up the contents of my stomach, that didn't mean the misery was over. I felt awful. God, I hated being nauseous. The cool porcelain felt good against my clammy skin. If I felt better, I'd cringe at the way I'd recently become BFFs with a toilet.

It had been two weeks since I'd been transported back to Earth. Two weeks since Warden Egara found me unconscious on the transport pad. She'd been stunned to see me. From my perspective, I'd only been on Trion for two days. But according to some really messed up space-time weirdness I didn't understand, eleven weeks had passed on Earth. Eleven weeks since she'd transported me off planet to my new mate, to Roark. She'd assumed I was successfully settled. Perfectly matched.

Happy.

And I had been, for a few hours at least. But the two weeks since my return had felt like forever. For two weeks I waited for Roark to come for me. Yes, the doctor had said he was dead when the Drovers attacked the guards, but I hadn't believed her. Roark had said he'd come for me, that he'd be safe. He had promised me.

And yet, time passed and I was alone. No word was sent

through the Brides Processing center to me, no messages arrived from Trion. Warden Egara gave me her word she would contact me immediately once she heard news of Roark.

I had called her every day and...nothing. No news. The warden had even sent a request for information to their planetary government. All they would tell her was that there had been a slaughter at Outpost Two with no survivors.

No survivors, except me.

I alternated between being mad and sad. Mad that he'd left me, that he'd chosen to take care of his parents instead of me. He'd put me second, protecting his parents and the people of the camp, pushed me away to take care of more important things. He'd behaved exactly the way I'd come to expect from the people in my life. Just like my parents. I was their child and they just shoved me in boarding school so I didn't interfere in their lives. Like my stupid fiancé, Curtis, who'd fucked others because he didn't want to take the time to know me, or bother to learn about me or what would make me happy.

When the anger drained me of energy, I switched to despair. I hated Roark, was so very angry at the thought that he was dead. I'd kept the hope alive that he'd come, that I could yell at him, tell him how mad I was and then kiss him senseless.

But after fourteen days, I stopped lying to myself. He wasn't coming. He was dead.

I'd even called my parents—who I'd tracked down to a villa in Sardinia—to tell them I was back on Earth. They'd been confused at first, wondering when I'd ever left. Apparently they never found the note, never even knew I'd been several light years away getting it on with a hot space alien. They hadn't cared, only asked if anyone knew about my return.

They didn't speak the word *failure*. They didn't need to. Everyone on the planet knew that brides never came back. Except me.

Always, I disappointed them. They obviously didn't know that Warden Egara used to be a bride and that she, too, had returned a widow. I hadn't bothered to enlighten them. All of it was irrelevant. They had never really cared what was going on with me. They still didn't.

They weren't even coming home to Boston, instead continuing on with their three-month tour of the Mediterranean through winter. Be back in March, they said. Can't wait to see me, they said. Welcome to stay in any of their homes, they said.

I was like a pet, not a daughter.

I was alone and angry and hurting. And the bitch of it was, I was also pretty sure I was pregnant. With an alien's baby.

God, my mother would fucking *love* that. I'd have to make up an Earth fling. If they knew the child growing inside me wasn't human, they'd freak. Talk about not belonging at the country club.

Yes, I had to be pregnant. This wasn't the stomach flu, because after about an hour, and some saltine crackers, I felt fine. By lunchtime, I was ready to eat anything put in front of me, and this was the third day the vomiting had happened. And my period was late. Only a few days, but I knew. I was never late. My breasts hurt, ached and were painful to touch. They were even more sensitive. The nipple rings kept me constantly aroused—except when I felt like hurling—and the chain only made it all more intense. I couldn't count the number of times I'd made myself come with my fingers, thinking of Roark's thick cock.

I couldn't stop thinking about Roark. I had his rings, his chain that dangled between. I had the small knife he'd pressed into my palm, the golden blade that had saved my life. I had memories. I knew what it felt like to be wanted, to be claimed and caressed and loved until I couldn't see straight.

It was more than some girls ever got, and I tried not to hate him for making me fall in love with him and then dying.

One night of wild sex. One night and that was all his powerful Trion sperm needed to make me pregnant. To breed me. That was the word he'd used. He'd needed a bride to breed. Well, it worked. I had his gold, my memories, and a baby. *His* baby, growing inside me.

The tears fell then, plopping onto the cold, white edge of the toilet's rim. I had my hair tied back in a ponytail so it wouldn't fall into the water. If he were here, he could hold my hair for me while I puked. He could bring me water and crackers. He could pull me into his arms and tell me everything was going to be okay.

But he wasn't here. I'd never see him again.

Warden Egara had offered to put me through the bride processing protocol again. I could be matched to another warrior since Roark was presumed dead. I'd decided against it, my wounds too raw. The shock of my experience with Roark too painful. I needed time to process.

And now this.

I placed my palm low, over my abdomen, and wondered who was there. A little girl with my eyes and Roark's darker skin? A son with dark hair and eyes the color of chocolate? I imagined Roark's face in miniature from a baby boy and the tears streamed down my face in an uncontrollable flood.

I grabbed a tissue and wiped the wetness from my cheeks. God, hormones were a bitch. I had one night with my perfect man. One night where we'd committed ourselves to each other.

He'd promised. Promised! But no, he was gone. Left me

alone. Just like my parents, like Curtis, the asshole. Oh, we might be on the same planet again, but I knew now he really did have a pencil dick.

Warden Egara had been sympathetic when I said I wanted to stay nearby the Miami Transport Center to wait. She'd come to check on me every day and I felt a connection with her. She'd lost two husbands and knew how I felt, for she'd felt it even worse. She'd had more than one day to get to know her mates. And she'd had two Prillon warriors for mates. The sad story had come out of her in her efforts to console me. She'd suffered a double loss. If I felt this horrible after spending just a day with Roark, then I couldn't imagine how she got out of bed every day. How she breathed in and out. How she got on with her life.

She said I was the only Earth woman, besides herself, to go off-planet and return. Well, another woman who'd been matched to Trion *had* returned because she had to testify at a trial, but she'd gone back soon after. Warden Egara had said she was the High Councilor's mate and that they probably knew—no, had known—Roark. It was a small universe, it seemed.

The nausea rolled up again and I leaned over the toilet bowl, dry heaving. When the fit was over, I slumped down on to the floor and curled up in a tight ball on the sparse bath mat. I couldn't stay in the hotel any longer. I had to face the reality that Roark wasn't coming, that he was dead and I had to get on with my life. I didn't have the luxury of lying around feeling sorry for myself any longer. I had a son or daughter to care for, who would need me to keep my shit together.

A baby! Pressing a hand to my flat stomach, the tears welled up again. This was not how I was supposed to become a mother. Alone in a hotel room. No husband. Not on this planet or even this galaxy. I just couldn't bare the thought of entering the Interstellar Brides Program again. Not a chance. Even if I could find a mate who would want another man's child, I didn't want to be matched to someone else. My one perfect match was dead. Roark was dead.

I was alone. My one attempt at finding happiness for myself, for taking charge of my life, failed. Failed miserably. I was even more alone, more heartbroken than before. Before, my loneliness had been abstract, a vague emptiness. Now that empty space was filled with pain. Now, I knew exactly what I'd been missing.

Sitting up, I cupped my breast and fiddled with the nipple ring. I wanted it off. I wanted to rid myself of the constant reminder of what I couldn't have. But there was no seam, no way to remove it. Screeching in frustration, I slumped back to the floor, crying. My nipple now tingled and I needed to touch myself, to relieve the ache. Even with my tears, I reached between my legs and found myself wet and swollen, my clit hard. Turning onto my back, I parted my legs and slipped two fingers into my needy pussy as I fingered my clit. I thought of Roark, of his deep voice and huge cock filling me, stretching me open, making me scream. It didn't take long to come, so eager was my body for completion.

I arched my back and cried out his name as the pleasure overwhelmed me. And when it had waned, when I was lying on a hotel room floor, sweaty, naked and alone, I knew it was time to move on with my life. It was time to go home.

CHAPTER 9

I OPENED MY EYES. Blinked. Again. I heard my name.

"Roark!"

"Councilor."

I groaned as I was shifted and moved. Everything hurt and I couldn't get the stench of that damn *nox* hair out of my nose. And blood. Burned flesh. Pain. I smelled like pain.

"Lift him carefully. He'll need at least a full day in the ReGeneration Pod."

I saw nothing but white at first, then some colors mixed in, then everything came into focus. So did the face that loomed over me.

"He's waking up." Seton, my second-in-command, exhaled and gave me a grim smile. Seton was two years older than I, a trusted friend. His family bloodline traced back nearly as far as mine. As the last son of my line, I had been elected councilor. But we both knew if I failed to produce an heir, or was killed, the people would embrace my sister's son. But he was no more than a babe. An infant could not rule. Seton would be acting councilor until my nephew was old enough to put forth his name in the elections. And for that, I was grateful. I'd never truly believed that possibility needed to be considered. But I'd never been taken and tortured before. Without doubt, had I not escaped, they would have killed me. Eventually.

I tried to sit, but Seton's large hand landed on my chest and he shoved me, none too gently, back down onto the medical bed. "What happened, Roark? We lost contact with Outpost Two days ago. But the transport pad was locked, at least until you used it." Seton's gaze roamed over me from head to toe, rage and uncertainty equally visible in his gaze.

"Drovers." I bit out the one word, the pain behind it hot and bitter. I heard a rumbling of voices in response to my announcement. I turned my head and looked beyond Seton's large frame. I could make out more than a dozen men, most in medical uniforms, and a few, scattered guards.

Seton leaned in and lowered his voice. "Drovers? Attacking an outpost? Are you certain?"

I nodded grimly. "They attacked. Set off explosions. I sent Natalie off with the doctor for protection. I gathered the men to chase the attackers into the desert. But it was a trap, Seton." I sighed, realizing that both Natalie and my parents would be dead if they had remained with me, as they had wanted to do. "The Drovers didn't run—they invaded the camp on foot."

"Drovers never leave their beasts," Seton insisted. "It's suicide."

"They were heavily armed and fought like trained warriors. I was trying to get to Natalie when I was ambushed and captured." I cleared my throat as the memory flooded me. "They slit Byran's throat and left him to bleed out in the sand."

"I'm sorry, Roark. We found him among the dead."

"And Natalie? My parents? Did they get out in time?"

"Your parents transported to Xalia City nine days ago. We heard nothing from the outpost, knew nothing of anything wrong until your arrival. I've sent scouts to the outpost to search for survivors. They're sending updates every fifteen minutes."

"What day is today?"

He told me and I thought back.

Nine days. The Drovers held me for eight and I rode a *nox* back to the Outpost for another. *Fark*. Where was Natalie? What could she have done in all this time?

"Natalie!" I shouted.

"Roark, calm down. Who is Natalie?" he asked. He was big and dark like me, like almost all Trion males, but somehow he was born with pale eyes. They were very noticeable and he didn't lack for attention with the females. He had yet to mate, probably enjoying the variety of willing bed partners who threw themselves at him.

"My mate." I hissed out a breath as I was lifted onto a stretcher, their hands on my back and ribs like knife blades, and someone jolted my twisted knee.

"Careful!" Seton shouted.

"I need to find her. Where is she?" Lifting an arm, I grabbed Seton's shirt. I could see ReGen wands passing over me as I was carried from the transport room. I didn't even remember arriving at the transport pad in Sector Two. The foul-smelling *nox*, the sand, the heat. The pain. It was all a blur. A painful blur. I remembered stumbling into the tent. Seeing blood in the sand. The control panel…

His eyebrows went up. "You claimed a female?"

"An Earth female. She's mine. Where is she?"

Seton continued, seeing I was anxious. "All I know is your parents transported to Xalia nine days ago. No other transports came here from Outpost Two until you showed up a few minutes ago, half dead. You somehow transported here, to Outpost Nine.

I leaned my head back and closed my eyes. Gods take it. I was on the Northern continent, in High Councilor Tark's territory.

Of course Seton was here. I'd sent him to Tark two months ago to work out Drover protection schedules over trade routes in the West, a duty Tark and I shared.

"How the *fark* you did it with your injuries, I have no idea." Seton looked down my body and watched as the doctor tried to work on me. We'd stopped moving but I couldn't see around all the bodies that circled me. I had no idea where I was, exactly. I had to assume they'd carried me to the medical station.

"Get me the leader of your guards," I said, my voice loud and commanding. "Now!"

The head guard, a commander, pushed his way between attendants, bowed to me. His uniform and insignia indicated his high rank. "I'm Commander Loris. It is good to see you alive, Councilor." While his words were well wishes, his tone was anything but happy as he saw the extent of my wounds. "Your injuries indicated you'd been tortured."

"Mmm," I murmured, thinking of what the Drovers had done to me. That was nothing compared to what I felt now. Out of control. Frustrated. The pain was lessening with whatever the doctors were doing, but it wouldn't soothe the need to search every corner of the planet for Natalie. "They did not attack as usual."

"They kept you alive, you mean?" Commander Loris asked.

"Exactly. It is not their usual behavior. Why did they not just kill me with the others?"

Seton cleared his throat. "There have been a number of cases in the North, Councilor, where they have taken high-ranking officials and tribal leaders and demanded a ransom."

"And did they demand a ransom for me?"

"No. It's safe to assume they didn't realize who you were when they took you."

I dropped my head back onto the stretcher and closed my eyes. "They would never release a councilor."

"Exactly." Seton's hand landed on my shoulder with a gentle squeeze. "You'd be too dangerous an enemy."

If they'd touched Natalie, if they'd hurt her, they had no idea how terrible an enemy I'd become.

"Where is my mate, Seton?"

"As soon as you were cleared from the transport pad, I sent a group of guards to Outpost Two." He looked away for a moment, then back. "It's only been an hour, but they are reporting back complete carnage, as you know. Typical Drover actions. They have yet to find any survivors."

"My mate was there."

His cool demeanor slipped, his eyes widened. I watched as his jaw clenched. "What does she look like?"

"She is beautiful." With my eyes still closed it was easy to picture her, as I'd been doing during my captivity. "Golden hair and pale eyes, like yours, but blue." The bluest eyes, the softest smile, lush curves, pert nipples adorned with little rings, a pink pussy.

"I'll find her." Seton patted my shoulder as the doctor stepped forward and I opened my eyes to look at him, to judge the veracity of his vow. He meant what he said, and I nodded. He was a good man. A good friend.

"I'm sorry to interrupt, but we need to get you into the ReGeneration Pod. You're bleeding internally, sir."

Fark.

"You're no good to your mate, or your people, if you're dead," the doctor insisted.

Gods damn all doctors for stating the obvious and being asses about it.

"I'm sorry, Councilor." The commander cleared his throat, his hand to his ear as if he were actively listening to an incoming message. He started to speak, stuttered, as if the next words were getting stuck. "I...They said they've found a woman dead in the transport center." He cleared his throat again but did not tell me anything more.

"How do I know it's her?"

Commander Loris walked to the side of the room, mumbling too low for me to hear. I waved the doctor off when he moved forward, the intensity of my glare enough to inform him that I wasn't going into the healing pod, not yet.

The commander stepped toward us again, his expression more grim than just a moment ago. "Councilor." He swallowed slowly, the slow movement of his throat and refusal to meet my gaze caused my pulse to pound in alarm. "They also found a cream-colored dress coated with blood."

My heart skipped a beat, then roared in my chest. Natalie. Natalie had been wearing that dress when we walked out of Mirana, looking beautiful and flushed, her skin glowing with health, her eyes dancing with happiness. No. Gods no.

"How did she die?" My voice cracked and fire burned in my eyes. I would kill them all. Every fucking Drover on the entire southern continent. The commander's gaze was filled with pity, which only served to make me angrier. "How. Did. She. Die?"

He glanced at Seton, who nodded almost imperceptibly.

"Stabbed in the back, sir."

My vision became fuzzy and the doctor yelled with

alarm. "Get him into the Pod! Now! Or we're going to lose him."

Seton assisted the medical staff as they lifted me from the stretcher into the ReGen Pod. The commander followed alongside us, pausing, listening to a voice coming through his communication device. "They've completed their search of Outpost Two."

"And?" Seton turned to him. Everyone stopped moving as the commander took a deep breath. My gaze drifted over the medical staff, Seton and the doctor as the commander tried to find the words we all already knew.

"Nothing but bodies, sir. I'm sorry. The sand and the flesh beetles have made it nearly impossible to identify the victims without DNA analysis. But the search crews say it won't matter, Councilor. I'm sorry. If your mate was at Outpost Two, she's dead."

Dead. My Natalie. My beautiful mate. Her body eaten away by the scavengers of the desert, the large, orange beetles that could pick a *nox*'s bones clean in a matter of days.

"No!" I bellowed, trying to sit up, then hissing in pain. Alarms sounded and the doctor cursed.

"Calm down, sir. You're bleeding heavily. Your heart can't take much more."

One of the others, a medical assistant in green, stepped forward. "He's bottoming out, Doctor. His heart is going to stop."

"*Fark*, Roark! Hold still!" Seton shouted at me and I relented because my body betrayed me, too weak to support my rage. Seton took full advantage, turning to the doctor. "Activate the pod now." He turned back to me, his pale eyes blazing with emotions I did not have the presence of mind, nor the concern, to name. "We'll make them pay, Roark. I promise you. But you can't hunt your mate's killers if you're dead."

"Do it." I stopped fighting, let the rage turn cold and hard inside me as I held the doctor's gaze. "Twelve hours."

"But, sir. My apologies. I highly recommend you remain in the pod for a full cycle. Your wounds are extensive." The doctor wrung his hands and I shook my head.

"No. Twelve hours. No more." Twelve hours and I would return to Outpost Two with a thousand men, and rain fire down on the Drovers until the ache in my heart eased, or until I was dead.

Multiple sets of hands had transferred me to the soft, cocoon-like structure to be healed. I watched as the walls came up all around me, sealing me inside a ReGen Pod. The doctor's concerned face was clearly visible through the odd blue glass above my face. He adjusted the controls on the side of the pod as the doctor began the healing cycle.

"Natalie." I spoke her name softly, reverently, like my own personal prayer. I was sure they all could see the anguish in my eyes.

Seton leaned forward so I could see his face through the glass. "I will transport to Outpost Two myself and search for her while you recover. You have my word that all efforts will be made to find out exactly what happened."

"Leave him be. He needs to heal, and he's already fighting the pod." The doctor nudged Seton out of my view and I stared, unseeing, straight ahead. Pale yellow lights surrounded me and I knew I would be rendered unconscious for the healing in a matter of seconds.

I looked to Commander Loris, thoughts and orders spinning in my mind. Where to search. Who to take. Weapons procurements. Hunting grids. I opened my mouth to issue the orders, but the only word that came from my lips before the pod took over my body's energies was her name.

* * *

NATALIE

THE CONSTANT, electrical hum of the baby monitor on the kitchen counter was both comfort and distraction as I polished off the grilled cheese and tomato soup the cook had prepared for lunch. I sat in the kitchen at a small, round table where the servants came and went, stopping for a quick bite and a bit of gossip. It was the same table where I'd eaten most meals as a child, more orphan than Montgomery, sent to the country when I came home from school so as not to interfere with their parties and schedules in the city.

Although, they did usually send for me at Christmas, dress me up like a princess and parade me through a string of children's parties with fat, rosy-cheeked Santas with the other rich, pampered children.

I'd looked at each of those children in turn and wondered if their lives were like mine. If their parents actually cared, or if they, like me, were simply ornaments to be displayed at certain times of year.

"Stop it." I spoke the order to myself and glanced at the monitor. My little one still slept, his normal two-hour nap the only time I had to do anything for myself. I refused to allow the staff to care for him, to hold him, feed him or bathe him. He was mine and he was loved.

And he was going to feel that love every moment of every day of his life. I was going to be the one constant in his life. He would never wonder about his parent's love as I had. He might only have one, but I had enough love for him.

With a sigh, I stood and carried my plate and empty bowl to the giant white porcelain sink. Susan, the cook, nodded her thanks from where she stirred tonight's supper, a delicious-smelling, homemade, chicken noodle soup.

I thanked her for lunch and grabbed the monitor, heading

for my bedroom. I had a stack of Noah's clothes in a basket on my bed, waiting to be folded. Miranda, the maid, said she would do them for me, but I had declined.

I liked to bury my nose in his little clothes, hold them to my face and inhale the sweet baby scent of my son. He smelled like home to me. Like love.

Walking out of the kitchen, I passed the adjoining room without even glancing inside. I had no need to see the formal dining room where I'd taken so many meals alone. The table beyond was long, polished mahogany, and large enough to seat twenty. An elaborate chandelier hung low over the center. The chairs were high-backed and stiff, just like my parents.

I wondered how they ever got down and dirty enough to have a child in the first place. I couldn't fathom it. Perhaps I was the product of in-vitro fertilization. I could imagine my mother in a sterile doctor's office more than in the throes of passion, opening her body to her lover, taking what he offered, demanding more.

And just like that, my thoughts went up in flames. Roark. Always, when my mind drifted to my mate, my body would grow hot and needy, the ache between my legs very real. But nothing compared to the immediate ache that overtook my heart.

He was dead. He had to be. I'd waited for him for a long time, hoping. Hope had kept me going through the pregnancy. Hope that he'd come for me, as he'd promised. Hope that he'd survived the brutal Drover attack, even after Warden Egara told me otherwise.

But days turned into weeks. Weeks turned into months, then a year. Our son grew in my womb and came into the world, screaming and fighting. And still, my mate was gone.

Warden Egara's inquiries turned up nothing new. Outpost Two was lost. No survivors.

Roark was gone. Warden Egara said she could go to the Interstellar Coalition, to someone called The Prime, on the planet Prillon, the guy in charge of the whole Coalition, and ask for an exception for me and Noah. Ask for another mate on Trion.

I didn't want another mate. My heart was broken enough. Roark had been mine, my perfect match. My one true love. I'd felt the bond between us instantly and I'd given him everything, heart and soul and body. I had nothing left to give another mate. Noah was the only thing that mattered to me now. I had nothing left for a new man. Nothing.

But, luckily, I didn't need a mate to survive. I didn't need, nor want for, anything. When my parents heard about the baby, they'd deeded this property to me within forty-eight hours. I had unlimited access to multiple bank accounts filled with more money than I could spend in three lifetimes. For me, they said. So I would be secure, they insisted.

But we all knew the truth.

The house wasn't in the heart of Boston, where my parents' main residence was. The country home was more than a hundred miles outside the city, with fresh air and horses and none of my parents' friends, colleagues, country club acquaintances, or business associates within miles. An illegitimate grandchild—and they'd not accepted my mating as a true legal joining—was one thing.

An alien's offspring was another.

Better to keep me and little Noah—a grandchild they'd yet to meet—hidden from the rest of the world. If I had all the money I needed, a place to live, I wouldn't rock the boat. I wouldn't complain. I'd remain invisible as I always had.

I hurried up the stairs, my bare feet and loose hair a freedom I'd given myself since my time with Roark. My mother would not approve, insisting shoes be worn at all times, unless one was in bed. But I no longer cared what my mother thought, what she did or where she went. I only cared about my son.

The upstairs hallway, once filled with vases and priceless works of art, had been stripped bare on my orders. I'd spent a lifetime trying not to touch anything, break anything, tiptoeing around my own home like an invader.

Noah would not live that life. He was not yet four months old, but he would be crawling soon, and I would make this house his playground. Everything would be baby-proof and made safe for him to explore.

He would feel safe and comfortable. He would have the childhood I did not.

My bedroom was beautiful, the pale-cream-and-gold carpeting, the chocolate-brown silk on my bed. A large canopy was draped in brown and white, creating a protective cocoon for me to sleep in.

I walked to the edge and sat next to the laundry basket I'd left a few hours ago. The scent of fabric softener and baby drifted to me, and I smiled. A few steps away, the door to Noah's adjoining nursery stood slightly ajar. Just a crack, but enough that I could hear his little body rustling and moving as he woke from his nap.

Unable to resist, I went to him. His nursery was not the usual, animals going two-by-two or big, cuddly bears. Noah was special, and I wanted him to know where he came from.

Three walls were covered with stars and constellations. On the fourth, just above his head, I'd paid an artist to paint Roark's symbols, the crossed swords that represented Noah's father, and the symbol of his family, in two matching shields.

The servants hadn't asked, and I didn't offer to explain. I'd taken photos of the medallions that still dangled from the chain between my breasts with a cell phone and given them to the painter when she arrived.

The woman simply nodded and transformed the wall

above Noah's crib into both art and tribute in a dark, rich, gold-colored paint. Above his sweet head hung a mobile of the sun and moon that played *"Twinkle Twinkle"* when I pushed the button. Stored in my bedroom, in the nightstand drawer, was everything I had been able to find on the planet Trion. It wasn't much, but Warden Egara had helped, and I had photos of his home world, of the people who looked like he did, with their olive-toned skin, black hair and intense stares. I knew Noah would grow up to be big like his father. He'd weighed nearly ten pounds when he was born, and was so long he'd been lean despite the weight. He'd needed extra feeding to keep up with his growth and I'd quickly embraced the bottle as a way to feed his insatiable appetite.

Noah looked like his father, and yet he didn't. My son had thick black hair and olive skin. But his eyes were mine. Dark blue when he was born, instead of growing darker, as I'd expected, his eyes had grown paler by the day, matching my pale blue. The contrast in his coloring was striking already, and I knew, someday, I would be chasing girls away from him and his exotic looks.

But for now, he was mine. "Hey, big guy."

His eyes opened and he saw me. Just like that, he smiled, his chubby little cheeks bunching and his eyes sparkling with unfiltered joy.

Love rushed through me, so strong and fierce I could barely contain it. I reached for him, lifting him from his crib. I placed him on the changing table, dealt with a wet diaper quickly. He kicked and fidgeted, eager to get on with it as I laughed and blew raspberries on his soft little belly.

These were the moments when I rejoiced in my time on Trion.

Late at night, alone in bed, I missed him still. My mate. Roark. Being with Noah brought a little of Roark into the room.

Determined not to ruin the day, I leaned over and pressed my lips to Noah's soft belly again, blowing air in a loud, silly stream on his petal-soft skin. He kicked and squealed, his chubby little fingers brushing the bare skin of my stomach where he'd found an opening under my soft cotton T-shirt. My jeans were comfortable and well worn, and only one size larger than what I'd worn before. Not too bad.

I leaned over and made wild, growly noises as Noah squealed and kicked.

But then the fun stopped. Noah's hand wrapped around the gold chain that hung from my nipples and he tugged. Hard.

"Ouch!" With a chuckle, I lifted my shirt and found his chubby little fist clutched around the medallion in the center, the one his father had given me. "Let go, silly. That's not for you, baby. That belongs to Mommy."

I pried his fingers from the medallion, one by one, but his grip was surprisingly strong as he tried to pull the pretty, sparkling gold to his mouth.

"Noah!" His eyes sparkled with innocent delight as he quickly shoved the medallion into his mouth, fist and all, smothering the entire thing in drool. Which just made prying individual fingers free of the thing without hurting myself that much more difficult.

When I'd first arrived on Earth, I'd tried to remove the chain and the rings. I'd tried pliers and wire cutters. Everything I could think of, but nothing worked. Only surgery would remove them and I had no intention of going there. After a month or two, I'd grown used to them. Before Noah was born, it was my reminder of the short time I'd had with Roark. Then Noah replaced the chain and its medallions as a token of what we'd shared, for our love made him.

The chain remained my personal torment and pleasure, my one true connection to the man I'd loved and lost.

With infinite patience, and a strong desire not to have my nipples yanked on like that again, I finally got the wet, drool-covered medallion from his chubby little fingers.

"You are in trouble, mister." I shoved the gold back under my shirt and quickly tucked in the front, so his wandering hands could not find it again. "Come on, love. Let's go get something to eat."

I lifted him into my arms and made my way down the stairs, my son nestled snuggly under my chin.

CHAPTER 10

$\mathcal{R}$*oark, Outpost Nine, Northern Continent*

AFTER TWELVE HOURS in the ReGen pod, I was, per the scanners, ninety-two percent well. I had some bruising, some cuts that were pink, newly healed flesh. I wasn't perfect, as I would be if I had remained in the pod the recommended time. But I didn't have time to heal fully. I needed to know what happened to Natalie. If she really was dead, I needed to know. I couldn't rest until I knew the truth. How could I relax when she might be on Trion somewhere, lost, hurt, alone. The Drovers could have her now, torturing her as they had me. Tormenting her. Causing her pain.

I had to find her. And if I found a body, I would not rest until the DNA test confirmed the remains belonged to my mate.

I'd given her my word, my promise to come for her, to protect her, and I would honor that vow to my dying breath.

"You must give up. Let go," my mother said, coming into

my tent. I sat behind my desk, staring at the search grids for Outpost Two, reading reports of the attack. Outpost Nine was bigger than Two, the small desert outpost where, even now, my mate's body might be lying in the sand. There was no chance of an attack here. The tent community surrounding Outpost Nine had turned into a city within the desert. When High Councilor Tark was matched to his mate, she'd transported here.

I never imagined the danger Natalie would face simply transporting to the smaller, less-secure outpost. There had not been a direct Drover attack in years. Still, I should have known better, thought of all the consequences, the dangers. She was my mate and her safety should have been my highest priority. Not my convenience.

I never should have risked her. I should have waited until my return to Xalia, where a thousand men would have protected her night and day in the palace. I'd been impatient and eager. My lack of self-discipline had cost me everything.

And here my mother stood, with a frown on her face and a list of replacement females, insisting I now choose a mate from the capital. My mother was ready for me to move on. Ten days, and I was to forget the only woman I'd ever allowed into my heart.

I didn't turn to face my mother as I responded, afraid she would see my rage. She was my mother and I would offer her nothing but respect. But I was not a boy to be led around by my ear. I was a Councilor. I would not be forced to do anything. When my mother refused to listen, I made the only argument I knew would sway her. "Would you give up Father so easily? Your one true match?"

"That's different, son."

"No. It's not. You were his bride, Mother. Matched through the same system that gave my Natalie to me. She was my match. Perfect for me in so many ways. I claimed her. That very first night."

"It was only one night, Roark. Surely, if you would spend one night with—"

"No." Give up Natalie? *Never.* "There is no confirmation that she's dead."

"They found her dress."

"It's not enough. I can't give up so easily." I rose from my desk and came to stand before her. "I gave her my heart, Mother. Give me some time to heal."

My mother was quiet long enough to think she would not respond. "No. I would not be able to give up your father. I am sorry. I did not realize what she meant to you. I only saw her for a brief moment and she was not even awake. It is easy to dismiss her very existence, although I see now how much you long for her."

"I admit, I was skeptical, but the match…it was perfect. I want—"

My father ducked into the tent then, his eyes wide, his face full of… something I couldn't determine.

"Commander Loris is here. There's been a ping on your medallion. It's been activated." He was breathing hard, as if he had just run a great distance. I knew differently and it could only mean he was excited.

I straightened, renewed strength in my limbs, although I hadn't even realized I'd been weighted down with frustration, longing and despair. "What?"

Crossing the room, I joined my father, my mind spinning with questions. Possibilities. Hope.

He angled his head out the doorway. "Come, son. He's in the command center."

"A ping? I thought you wore your medallion about your neck?" My mother questioned.

While I should have let them lead, as a courtesy, I could

not wait. I almost pushed my father out of the way and ran out of the tent. The sand kicked up beneath my feet and I squinted at the bright double sunlight. In the entry of the command center stood the commander, the one I recognized from the day before.

"You have news." I didn't form it as a question.

Commander Loris gave a curt nod. "Central command in Xalia sent an urgent alert. Your medallion has been activated. I was sent immediately to ensure your safety. Although, seeing you, I will inform them that there must be a malfunction, as you are obviously alive and well."

My heart rate accelerated, my fingers itched to grab something. Anything. "I don't have the medallion. I gave it to Natalie."

"Natalie? Your mate? You gave it to her?" The commander stood, wide eyed. "Why would you do such a thing? Do you have any idea the value of that medallion to this planet?"

I knew he wasn't trying to be disrespectful, but I still couldn't hesitate to speak in a sharp tone of voice. "Yes, quite aware. Do you have any idea the value Natalie holds for me? She is the mate of a councilor, commander. I'd advise you to watch your tone with me."

He shifted to a formal ready stance, focused and fixed his gaze over my shoulder. "I apologize, Councilor."

"At ease, Commander." I stepped past him then and into Outpost Nine's command center.

Within the large tent were three guards. They stood and bowed at my arrival. Based on their uniforms, the commander was the highest ranked man in the room.

If the medallion pinged, then that meant—

"She's alive," I said to myself, my heart pounding, eagerness making me ready to rip the tent flap open and go get her, wherever the hell she was. I knew everyone watching me pace back and forth across the tent.

"Only your DNA can activate the medallion, councilor, not hers." The commander paused.

"She had the medallion."

"That doesn't mean she's alive," the commander countered. "Only that someone in your family has the medallion now."

My father stepped forward. "Other than you or I, your sister and her children are the only living members of the family who could unlock that medallion." I hadn't seen him enter the tent, but he spoke true. "Your sister is with her husband and High Councilor Tark. There's no chance Natalie ended up with them. Tark would have notified us."

"How could she have gotten there? Or known who Sari was?" my mother added, referring to my sister, Sari. And it was true. I'd never mentioned either High Councilor Tark or my sister to Natalie. Everyone looked baffled. The three guards manning the communications units remained silent. It was clear they were messengers and could offer nothing additional.

"Your speculation is irrelevant. The ping didn't come from Trion," the commander added.

I spun and faced him. "No one leaves this tent until I have answers. Commander, what, exactly, are you talking about?"

He took a deep breath. "The transport monitors received the activation from your medallion a short time ago. But the signal didn't come from Trion, sir. It came from Earth."

I stilled. "Earth?" *Natalie.*

I looked to my parents who appeared doubtful. My mother scowled. My father kept his features carefully blank. "That's impossible."

"I don't have an explanation, sir," the commander continued. It was my fault to have interrupted him. "The monitor in Xalia City notified us once the transmission codes were confirmed. There does not appear to be a malfunction. They are confident your medallion is on Earth."

"Natalie must be alive." My mother lifted her hand to cover her mouth, shock evident in the slight tremble of her fingers.

"But how would she activate the medallion?" my father asked the obvious question. I had no answers. Turning to Commander Loris, I demanded more information. "Did my mate somehow escape the Drovers' ambush by transporting to Earth? Why was there no log of the transport when Outpost Two was searched."

Commander Loris took a deep breath. "The transport station was locked, Councilor. It's data erased. The only transport code on file was yours. The only reason we have the transport codes for Earth are because High Councilor Tark's mate is also from the planet and your mates came from the same brides processing center."

Natalie. Alive. "Why didn't she return to me? Why didn't the transport station on Earth contact me?" What the *fark* was going on?

I knew I was rambling a bunch of questions no one could answer. No one but Natalie. She was mine, and a legal citizen of Trion. She was a matched mate. She belonged to me. If she was alive, I would not stop until I had her back in my arms, and in my bed, where she belonged.

I stalked toward the door and yelled for the nearest guard to contact Seton. I would leave him in charge of the southern continent during my journey. He would offer to accompany me, without doubt. But with the Drover threat looming, I needed him here. He would have to leave at once and return to the south. High Councilor Tark and the Drover patrols would just have to wait until I could bring my mate home.

Confident my orders would be carried out, I returned to the transport room and walked onto the transport pad.

"Contact the transport station on Earth. I'm going to get my mate."

* * *

NATALIE, *Near Boston, MA, Earth*

I ANSWERED the doorbell with Noah on my hip. I'd just changed his diaper and had yet to put his pants back on. Instead, he only wore a onesie and I loved looking at the rolls of fat on his chubby little thighs. He held a set of plastic keys in his tight fist and spent equal time shaking them and shoving them in his mouth.

When the door swung open, I sighed. I was so not in the mood for Curtis. Every time I saw the gaunt man I wondered what the hell I had been thinking. What had I *ever* seen in him? His hair was brown and thin, receding at an alarming rate and looked wet from a recent shower. He was pale and his cheeks were a bit swollen, as if he was retaining water. Medicine? Too much salt in his caviar? He wore a white golf shirt that had tiny pink lobsters embroidered on the sleeves. Khakis hung on his thin frame like a loose paper sack. He wore scuffed loafers without socks and a designer watch on his left arm that cost more than most people made in a month. There was nothing, not one thing, appealing about the man. No wonder I never had an orgasm with him. It would have been a miracle if that had occurred. Not to mention that he wore enough cologne to make me feel light-headed and nauseous.

My tolerance for smell had not improved since Noah's birth. I had a new superpower. Since the moment I'd become pregnant, I would swear I could smell a piece of red meat at twenty paces. I had really hoped my sensitivity to smells would go away once the baby was born, but no such luck. I tried not to gag on the scent of cedar and musk and opened the door wider, not to let my visitor in, but hoping for some fresh air.

"Curtis," I said on a sigh. I'd hoped the doorbell meant the plumber had arrived, for one of the faucets had burst in the kitchen and shot water out like Old Faithful every time the cook tried to use the sink. "This is a surprise."

Over the past year, Curtis had appeared on various occasions, unannounced and unwanted. He'd made his disinterest clear before I volunteered for the brides program. Upon learning of my return—no, upon my parents deeding me the large house—he'd resumed his interest in me.

"How's Mandy?" I asked about his sister, because that was truly the only safe topic of conversation open to me. I didn't want to know why he was here. I was not concerned about his life, his day, or his revived interest in me.

He didn't look at me, but at Noah. The look most people gave the baby was a soft smile, a gentle sigh, because my son was so damn cute. Who didn't like a baby? No one, but Curtis. It wasn't just that Noah was a baby. It was that Noah was a space alien's baby. At least that was how Curtis, and my parents, referred to Roark. A space alien. Not a respected leader of almost half a planet in the Interstellar Coalition. Not my mate. An alien.

"I came to see if you would attend the Winter Ball with me at the country club."

He didn't wait to be invited him in, just barged past me into the foyer. It was two-stories tall with a circular staircase and I knew it held more interest to him than I did. But I let it go and closed the door behind him, not because I welcomed him into my home, but because Noah's chubby little legs were bare, and it was cold outside.

"No, thank you, Curtis." I stepped around him and transferred Noah to my opposite hip. He was a big baby, and my biceps felt the strain. He definitely took after his father in size. "If that's all, I need to put Noah down for a nap." I needed him to know he was not staying long. Shouting might startle Noah and, at the moment, my son was content with his keys.

"I want you to wear the pink gown you bought for our engagement party."

Now, I did roll my eyes. That god-awful mass of lace, tulle and sequins? No. No way. Not in a million fucking years. I hated the thing the day my mother brought it home, and I hated it still. "I've told you before and I'll tell you again, I'm not interested. Ask Ashley, or Bambi. Whatever the name of your latest conquest is."

He turned his gaze from the chandelier that dangled from the ceiling, one thing Noah couldn't grab hold of and hurt himself with—and then looked at me. "They meant nothing, not when we were together. Not now."

"Oh?" Sounds like he still had women on the side, the bastard. "I'd think you'd want the woman you're fucking to mean something," I countered.

This conversation was getting old.

"What kind of mother are you, spewing foul language in front of a child?"

"Now you are concerned about Noah?" I asked, my voice dripping with sarcasm. Hoisting Noah up, I snuggled him in closer on my hip, kissed his downy head. "He's four months old. I don't think he'll be cursing for few months yet." I walked to the door, purposely placed my free palm on the door handle. "You need to leave, Curtis."

"Come with me to the ball. Leave the baby with a babysitter, a maid, whatever. It's time you got out from under this whole baby obsession, went to parties again. You can't hide in this house forever."

"I'm not hiding, you asshole. I'm not interested." I turned the handle and pulled the door open. "Get out. And please don't come back this time."

Curtis's whining had worn down my last nerve. How had I spent so much time with this man?

He walked toward me slowly, looking at Noah with a gleam in his eyes that frightened me. "If it weren't for that alien brat, you wouldn't be acting like such a bitch, Natalie."

Now I was pissed. "Get the fuck out of my house. Now."

"I don't think so. Everything was fine until you came home pregnant. Get rid of him and we'll go back to the way things were."

Get rid of him? "Have you lost your mind? You're talking about killing an innocent child."

"An alien." Curtis stepped closer and I swung the door even wider, stepping out into the cold in my bare feet, into view of the surveillance camera outside my front door. I tucked Noah's legs under my arms the best I could, shielding him from the cold.

"We're on camera, Curtis. Get off my property. If I ever see you again, I'm calling the cops."

Curtis looked like he would argue further, but his eyes darted past me, a look of near panic taking over his features.

"Get away from my mate before I kill you."

I knew that voice. Heard that voice in my dreams. I gasped, felt every hair on my body stand on end. Slowly, I turned.

Roark. I couldn't speak, not even to whisper his name. I couldn't believe my eyes. He was here.

He was here.

He was alive!

"Who the hell are you?" Curtis asked, hands on his hips, as if this were his house.

Roark moved in front of me, blocking Curtis's view of my

body. "I'm Councilor Roark of Trion, Natalie's mate. And if you don't get the fuck away from her, right now, I will kill you."

"You can't. You'll go to prison. I'm Natalie's friend. She invited me here."

"You're a liar, Curtis. Just go," I snapped. I wasn't even looking at him, but at Roark.

Roark shifted, pushing me toward the entrance, back to the warmth and safety of the house. "I believe my mate ordered you to leave and never come back."

The word "ordered" was said with emphasis and I could just imagine Curtis's face turning red, his eyes bulging. I couldn't see him, not over the hulking mass of muscle blocking my view. Roark was so big, so handsome, so... everything. I'd forgotten how much larger than life he was. My heart pounded in my ears and I began to shake. My feet were going numb from the cold, but I didn't care. Noah, however, started to fuss, and I knew he must be getting cold. With Roark here, I didn't need to stand outside anymore. I didn't need to worry about Curtis or his slimy intentions.

"Go inside, *gara*. I will take care of this fool."

Nodding, I rushed into my house and headed for the study just inside the door. Inside, a cozy gas fireplace heated the room to toasty perfection and Noah's playpen and toys were already set out on the floor. Two short sofas made an L shape opposite the playpen, the soft navy suede a recent purchase I'd quickly grown to love. The cold leather I remembered from my childhood had been replaced with soft, squishy warmth. The room was cozy now, and mine.

Mine and Noah's.

I placed my son in his playpen and stood watching over him, my hands shaking. I ignored the sounds of confrontation outside. Ignored Curtis's shout of pain, his ranting and cursing as he walked to his car and sped out of the driveway.

I felt like I was in a dream, a fuzzy dream. When my mate stood in the doorway, looking down on me like a conquering god, the dream faded and he was all too real.

"Roark," I whispered. I couldn't make it any louder than that and I couldn't move.

"Do I need to be concerned about that Earth male?"

Roark's voice was all dark and possessive and I had to laugh. "Curtis? No. He's not a problem."

He wasn't. Never had been. And with Roark here, Curtis who?

Roark's eyes found mine. Held. Yes, that was the look I'd craved. Desperation. Need. Hunger. Love.

In three steps, he crossed to me, stood so close I had to tilt my chin back.

"You're not dead." It was a stupid statement, but that one thought consumed me as I drank him in with my eyes, afraid to touch him, afraid he'd vanish like a ghost. "The doctor told me you were dead."

Roark shook his head and gathered me close. His scent, god, his scent was fabulous. One that triggered every happy memory of the short time with him. His voice rumbled through his chest and into me as he explained. "I was captured. They held me for nine days before I could escape. Everyone at Outpost Two was gone. I transported to another outpost and they told there were no survivors. They told me *you* were dead." His grip was tight, too tight. My ribs felt like they might snap, but I welcomed the pain. It was real. He was real.

"You thought I was dead?" My voice was high, tight.

"Yes, *gara*." He breathed deep. "Gods help me, yes."

I shoved at his chest, fighting back the anger rising in my stomach, churning its way up my throat, into my head, leaking out my eyes. I would not cry, but these tears fell unbidden. "Nine days?"

He groaned "Ten now, love."

"Ten days?" I nearly shouted. "Ten fucking days? Is that supposed to be funny?"

Roark lifted a hand to my face and tucked a strand of hair behind my ear. How could he be so calm as he lied to me? "What is wrong?"

I shoved at his chest and stepped away, putting Noah's playpen between us. "You thought I was dead?"

"Yes."

"Then why are you here now? This is what, light years away? Why now?" How had he found me? Why was he here? Ten days? Hardly. I'd been alone and miserable for thirteen fucking months. I'd been pregnant, *alone* and scared. I cried myself to sleep every night for months. I'd grieved him for over a year.

Ten days? No. Not even close.

"You activated the medallion's emergency signal, mate. I don't know how you did it, but I was never so relieved as when that ping came through the transport center on Trion. I came at once."

What. The. Hell? "What ping?"

He stepped around the playpen, where Noah had rolled onto his side, busy shoving a crackling golden bear into his mouth. Was Roark really so dense? So confused? How could he not see that Noah was his son? He had not really looked at our son, at the small replica of the giant man before me. I wanted him to look. I wanted him to *see*.

"The medallion I gave you, *gara*. The one I put on your chain that night. When I claimed you, made you mine forever. It can only be activated by—" His voice faded and his attention focused wholly and completely on Noah for the first time. I'd wanted Roark to acknowledge his son, to *know*. To grasp the significance of that sweet, little face. But now that Roark's full attention was on the baby, I suddenly felt nervous.

I'd longed for this moment, wished it. Dreamed it. But now that it was happening, I was worried Roark wouldn't want Noah, wouldn't want me again. Us.

Roark's eyes clouded with wonder, with awe, and I watched the riot of emotions cross his face like a storm. *"Gara?"*

"It's been more than ten days, Roark," I whispered, the tears falling again. "A lot more."

He shook his head slowly. The truth was before him, but he couldn't seem to fathom it. "How… how is this possible?" By the way his fingers twitched, I could sense that Roark wanted to touch him, to hold him, yet was afraid. Shifting, I lifted Noah up so Roark could take him.

With wide eyes and big hands, he took Noah from me, pulled his son into his chest, snuggled him close. A groan escaped Roark's body, part joy, part pain, and the baby squealed in delight, smacking at his father's chest with his toy.

"Gara." Tears gathered in Roark's eyes when he lifted his glittering gaze to mine and the sight made my heart split in two. All the anger drained from me in an instant. I didn't know how or why Roark was here, or why it had taken him so long to find us. But he'd kept his promise. He'd come across the galaxy to find me, to find us. And the violent wrenching in my heart meant I loved him still.

"His name is Noah. He's your son."

CHAPTER 11

NATALIE WAS CURLED into my side. A fire burned in the strange hearth before us. But there was no fuel, no tree or brush feeding the flames. Still, it heated the room, and the little one who slept on my chest.

My son.

Just thinking the word caused my eyes to burn, my heart to ache. My son. And I'd missed so much already. My mate's rounded belly, the swell of her breasts. I'd missed his birth, his first smile.

My son did not know my face, my touch, my voice.

But his mother did. My mate melted into my side, soft and sweet and more beautiful than I remembered and it had only been ten days. Her face was slightly rounder, her luscious curves more pronounced. I could not wait to strip her naked and claim her once more, remind her that I was her master, just as she'd vowed. And yet, the small body resting with such trust, such vulnerability against my chest exerted his own influence, and I remained locked between them, powerless to resist.

"What took you so long, Roark?" My mate's arm draped over my body, just below our son.

"They held me prisoner, *gara*." The pain of those days felt distant now, as distant as Trion was from Earth, my new reality so overwhelming and vibrant that the time spent chained in that tent felt hazy. "I came for you, mate."

She tilted her chin up so her eyes met mine. "It's been thirteen months, Roark. More than a year."

A year? I shook my head. "I don't know how that is possible, Natalie. But we will get answers. For me, it has been just ten days. Eight days of torture. My escape. Half a day in the ReGeneration Pod. And then the medallion. You."

A soft sound escaped her throat and I turned my attention from the sleeping perfection of our son's round face to hers. "ReGeneration pod? They tortured you?"

"My apologies. I do not wish to cause you upset. It is over now. Of no consequence."

"Of no consequence?" Her fingers gripped my shirt. "It matters to me."

I should have kept my mouth shut, for I was a universe away from the danger on Trion. The Drovers couldn't harm either of us here. Noah, either. I wished my words hadn't made my little mate's fair face flush pink with outrage. Not only did she get up, moving away from me, she took my son from me and walked to the door. She called for a woman and asked her to take Noah to his crib and watch over him for a few hours. She was of similar age to Natalie and seemed to be a maid or childcare giver.

I stood then, ready to tell Natalie no, that I didn't want my son to go with anyone. I just had him in my arms and he was mine. I didn't want to ever let him go.

The woman, though, had a kind smile, and Noah nestled in her arms without waking. Natalie seemed to trust her and I must as well. It didn't make it any easier.

I could see the woman carrying Noah up the stairs through the open doorway. With Noah out of my sight, a small growl escaped.

Natalie closed the door and turned to face me. "Don't worry, she's just taking him to his room for his nap. She'll stay with him."

I nodded, knowing she was right, and relaxed my hands from the fists I hadn't realized I'd made. Noah would be fine while he slept.

She crossed her arms over the full swell of her breasts, eyed my body. "In the meantime, take off your clothes, mate. Now."

I arched a brow at her demands. I was not used to her being so commanding, so in control. I liked it. So did my cock.

I had no wish to argue. This was her world and she knew it better than I. She knew our son was safe and I would trust in her on that. She also knew we needed to settle some confusion between us. For her, a year's worth of confusion. If she wanted to do it while I was naked, I would not deny her.

The room was warm and comfortable, the rug on the floor before the hearth soft and thick, the perfect place to spread my mate wide and fill her with my cock. But I would let her have her way. For now.

I undressed quickly, not caring if she had meant for me to remove everything or not. My reward was there, in the quickening of her breath, the dark lust rising in her eyes as she inspected my body. Remembered.

She walked around me slowly, her fingers tracing the new, pink scars on my back, the wounds still not completely healed on my chest and thighs. My muscles flexed and I could barely breathe as she touched me gently. Reverently. "Why aren't you healed? I thought you guys had technology that could heal almost anything. God, were you hurt that badly?"

A shudder raced down my spine and my cock thickened, growing impossibly large. When she came around from behind me, she'd see it almost touched my navel. My balls were heavy, aching to fill her again. If fucking her for just one night made Noah, we could certainly do it again. "Now you sound like the doctors, mate." My voice was deep, rough with need.

"Answer the question."

"There was no time."

"No time?" Natalie walked to stand before me and I looked down into her upturned face, trapped by the need I saw burning in her bright blue eyes. "I don't understand."

"It would have taken long hours to heal completely." I raised my hand to her lovely face and traced her cheek with my fingertips. Her skin was as soft as I remembered. "But I refused."

"This is crazy, Roark. Why? Why wouldn't you let them heal you?"

"It had been ten days, mate. Ten days and they said you were dead. I was frantic. I had to find you, to know for sure. If you were out there, I had to get to you. And I did."

Natalie leapt into my arms and I caught her, tucked my hands under her ripe ass as she wrapped her legs around my hips. Her fingers threaded through my hair and pulled, hard, demanding I lower my head and kiss her. Her mouth was soft, her kiss hot and she was so responsive. She opened to me and I tasted her, my tongue tangling with hers.

She pulled back, her breath ragged. "God, it's been over a year."

I looked into her pale eyes, saw the passion and the need.

The truth. "I don't understand. It's been ten days and that was long enough. How could it be a year? I see proof of it in our son, but it makes no sense."

"Warden Egara said time isn't the same. I'd only spent just one night with you, but when I was transported back, it had been eleven weeks since I'd left Earth. Eleven!"

The reality of what happened settled heavily, like a *nox* had sat on my chest. "I'm sorry, mate. *Fark*."

What she must have felt to arrive back on Earth, alone, thinking me dead.

"I'm so glad you're here, but I'm so mad at you."

I brushed her wild hair back from her face. "Mad?"

She stepped away, looked down at the magical flames. "You left me to go to your parents." I heard the way her voice broke. "You chose them over me."

I went to her, spun her to face me. "Left you? I saw to your safety first." Didn't she know I would take care of her above anything else? By the hurt, angry look in her eyes, the answer was no.

She shook her head. "No. You sent me off with the doctor. You cared more about your parents. You worried for them, saw to their safety."

I closed my eyes, exhaled. "*Fark. Gara*, I didn't want you with me during the ambush because I couldn't guarantee your safety if you were by my side. I knew if you went with the doctor, you would be safe, protected."

She shook her head again, this time with lines of anguish on her face. "I wasn't safe. They died, Roark. The guards, the doctor. God, they died right in front of me. She put me on the transport pad just in case, then the Drovers came. It was the doctor who saved me."

She shuddered and I pulled her into my arms, held her tightly, her cheek pressed into my chest. I'd almost lost her.

Because of the doctor's smart planning, the guards that protected her, she was alive.

I spread my hand over her head, holding her to me so she would hear the words as they rumbled through my chest. "I vowed to protect you, Natalie. I sent you to the safest location in the Outpost. The one place I believed you would be safe."

She shook her head and I felt the hot sting of her tears on my bare chest. I lifted both hands to her cheeks and angled her head up, forced her to look into my eyes. "You are my mate, Natalie. I know you do not yet understand what you mean to me, but know this, I will always put you first. I will always protect you. I will always come for you."

Natalie bit her lip, her eyes clouded with doubt. "What about your parents?"

I lowered my forehead and pressed it to hers. "They are my family, *gara,* and important to me. But you are my heart."

"And Noah? What about him?" She sniffed and looked hopeful, cautious, and very protective of our son. All things a mother should be. I found I liked her fire, the intensity of her devotion to Noah. Seeing her as a fierce, loving mother only made me want her more. I could not wait to fill her with my seed, see her grow round with a second child. I wanted a girl next, with her mother's eyes. "What do you think about having a son?"

"He is the greatest gift anyone has ever given me, mate. I will love him and protect him with my life, as I will love and protect you. Always."

My mate studied me and I held her gaze, stood naked and vulnerable before her. For eight days I'd been tortured, but I knew my suffering was nothing compared to hers. I'd believed her dead for but a single day. She'd believed me dead for more than a year, gone through a pregnancy unprotected and alone. Raised our son on her own. Fought off unwanted male attention…

At least, I wanted to think she had not given her body to another. But with her beauty, her luscious curves, I had no doubt the sniveling fool here when I arrived was not the first man to want my mate.

"I want to take you home, Natalie."

"Back to Trion?"

"Yes. I want you home with me. There is so much I didn't get to show you, and Noah. The capital, Xalia, is a beautiful city, with gardens and markets, so much life. And the medallion I gave you is a key that unlocks a vault deep below the city."

"What?" She looked at me wide eyed. "You gave that to me?"

I nodded. "You are my mate. Of course you would have it. That's how I found you. The medallion. It only opens for my DNA. Noah touched it, didn't he?"

She thought for a moment and nodded.

"While you hold the key to the southern continent on your chain, Noah has the power to open it. He helped me find you again."

Warm air escaped her parted lips with a hint of a shudder. "What's in it?"

"Knowledge. Wealth. Power. The planet at your feet, mate. I gave you everything, love." I traced her bottom lip with my thumb, hungry to taste her. But I would not take her without her consent. "Come home with me."

* * *

Natalie

. . .

ALL THE MONTHS OF ANGUISH, of mourning, of anger, somehow seeped away, like water down the drain. Time hadn't been on our side. We'd only had a day together before we were ripped apart. While I'd known since I first transported back to Earth that time was different on Trion, I hadn't considered it might be the reason Roark had never come, why it had taken him so long. The doctor told me he was dead. I'd hoped, but I'd thought him dead, believed I'd never see him again. Time meant nothing when death was involved.

But for Roark, he'd come as soon as he could. God, he'd been captured, tortured and hurt enough to need the fancy pod medicine. I wanted to cry over what he'd gone through, but he was here and didn't seem to think it was important. As soon as he found out I was alive, he'd done exactly as promised. It had only been ten days for him. Ten! He'd rushed across the galaxy to me and discovered a sleazy man wearing lobsters in my entry and a baby on my hip. While I'd had plenty of time to adjust to having a baby, he'd only had a mate for eleven days. He'd been a father for an hour.

In such a short time, he'd gained a mate and a baby. I had to assume no other Trion male could make a baby in such a short time.

It was important for Roark to know his child, to bond with him after the months he'd missed, but Noah was asleep. It *was* time to revel in the knowledge that we still had each other. Seeing him, holding him, breathing him in wasn't enough.

I needed the connection we'd shared on Trion in the oasis. I needed to join with Roark so I didn't know where he began and I ended. I needed him inside me. Deep.

"Yes," I breathed, either in response to his words or to my thoughts of having him filling me up. Which didn't matter. I wanted both. I dropped to my knees, my hands sliding down his torso, over chiseled abs to rest on his rock-hard thighs. Directly before me, bobbing, was his cock. I licked my lips in anticipation of tasting him. The head was wide and plush, the color of it a ruddy red. Fluid seeped from the tip and made my mouth water. He was so long, I couldn't take all of him. A vein bulged down the throbbing length and I was eager for him, to feel him, taste him on my tongue. When I saw his fingers clench into fists, he was as needy as I. He was holding back all that coiled tension, that desperation.

I didn't make him wait any longer, but licked up the pre-cum on the tip, then opened wide and took him deep. He was warm and hard and thick and salty on my tongue. Beneath my palms, I felt his muscles tense. He groaned deep and his hand went to my head.

I wasn't that good at giving blow jobs, never found much appeal in them. Now? Now I wanted to take as much of Roark as I could, to swallow down every drop when I made him come.

"*Gara*." his fingers tightened and he pulled me farther onto him, then tugged me completely off.

I looked up his naked body to see his dark eyes fierce and wild.

"You are wearing too many clothes," he murmured. When I fumbled with my shirt, he reached down and stilled my hands. "Let me."

Kneeling down in front of me, he took hold of the hem of my shirt, lifted it slowly, his knuckles grazing along my skin. When I was before him in just a bra, he frowned. "What is this?"

I looked down at myself, my full post-baby curves lifted into plump mounds by the sturdy bra. It was white with lace edging, but very basic. I hadn't expected to be stripped bare by my mate when I got dressed this morning. While the bra contained my breasts well enough, the chain was wedged into my cleavage and dipped over the space between the cups.

"It's a bra."

Roark's big finger ran over the full swells, then hooked around the chain, tugging it up very gently from beneath the cotton.

"I wear one now because I'm... I'm bigger now after Noah."

"Yes, you are," he replied, not just noticing the size of my breasts, but my hips, everywhere I'd changed. His head angled from side to side. "How do you take it off?"

Reaching behind me, I unhooked it, let it slide off my shoulders and down my arms. My nipples hardened instantly and the chain pulled downward, making them so sensitive.

He cupped my breasts in his rough palms then. Yes, they were much bigger than before. I wanted to close my eyes, but I needed to see him, see the way his jaw clenched, his thumbs brushed over my nipples.

"They are heavy with milk," he added. Of course, he could tell the difference in them.

"Some," I replied, giving over to the pleasure of his hands. "Your son is a greedy boy and I don't have enough. He also drinks from a bottle."

When I felt the hot, wet heat of his mouth on my hard tip, I looked down, stared. He suckled gently, watched me as he did so. "Mmm, sweet. I am very jealous of my son, having these all to himself. I like the feel of the ring in my mouth, that you have them, that you won't ever forget who you belong to."

It was my turn to tangle my fingers in his hair. "I... I couldn't get it off. The rings, the chain, it's stuck."

"Of course, it is. You're mine. *These* are mine." He gave my breasts a gentle squeeze.

"I'm sure Noah will share them with you." I whimpered. "Roark, God, they're so sensitive."

"I wondered if you could come from me playing with them."

"Before?" I shrugged. "Now?" I bit my lip when he switched to my other breast. "Definitely."

"There is much we didn't get to do together. I want to do them all with you. To you. But now, I need to taste you again. I want you to come all over my tongue."

He may have been slow before now, even letting me have my way, but his pace quickened as he quickly rid me of my jeans—although he swore at the odd material and fit—and panties. I was spread wide and his mouth was on me before I could even cry out his name.

The man knew what to do with his tongue. Perhaps it was because it had been so long, perhaps it was because I'd been so damn horny, but I was quick to come. I wasn't complaining and I was sure I made Roark feel like the stud he was, but I was crying out his name and dripping all over his face in record time.

I was a panting, sweaty, happy mess when he kissed his way up my body.

"God, I missed that tongue of yours."

When he loomed over me, propped up with his hand, he grinned. His mouth was still wet, and his beard. I shouldn't even think about how sexy his beard was. "You only missed my tongue?"

Reaching between us, I took hold of his cock, gripped it with my fingers. Because it was so large, I couldn't get my fingers to touch. I remember being amazed by his size and I still was.

"It's been so long," I whispered.

He moved his hand away and settled himself between my thighs. His cock knew exactly where to go and nudged right up against my slick opening. "I'll be gentle." He slid in, parting me wide until I was completely filled. "At first."

My eyes fell closed and my body went from zero to sixty again, his cock nudging and stroking sensitive spots. He'd been the only man to find my G-spot and he knew just how to hit it with that big cock of his.

Bending my knees, I brought my legs up, higher, then higher still to take him deeper.

He rocked into me, slowly at first, but when I came again —how could I hold back when he felt so good and knew *exactly* what to do with his cock—he lost all sense of control. I could feel my inner walls ripple and pulse around him.

"Mine," he growled, leaning down to murmur in my ear. His chest pressed into mine, the feel of his body rasping over my tender nipples had me squeezing him deep within.

"Yes," I replied. "Come. Please, Roark, I need to feel you come. Fill me up. Please."

I wasn't past begging. I needed to know I could satisfy him. It made no sense, for I knew he was aroused by me, but his orgasm was the ultimate proof that he could find pleasure in my body. With me.

I felt him thicken and swell in me, his thrusts becoming harder. He hooked the back of my knee and opened me wider for him. The sounds of fucking filled the room. Slaps of flesh, whimpers, harsh breathing. The scent of it clung to our skin, mixed, melded just as we were.

"Natalie," he groaned as he held himself deep, filled me. Made me his again.

It was then that I cried, pulling him down so I could wrap my arms around him. He was just where I'd wanted him to be for so long. Over me, pressing me down with his solid weight. Him thick and heavy inside me. His seed seeping out. His heartbeat as frantic as mine.

He tried to soothe me, stroking my hair back from my

face, kissing me gently, but I kept on crying. When he shifted to his side and pulled me on top of him, our positions switched, he held me as the tears kept falling, his cock still deep inside. I let it all bleed away until it was just Roark and me again. And Noah, our son, the proof of our love.

 *atalie*

I WOKE IN BED, where Roark had carried me when the tears dried. Glancing at the bedside alarm clock, I saw that it was about four in the morning. It was still dark outside, and I was too comfortable to move. I snuggled into the heavy blankets, happier than I'd ever been. Roark was here, with me. With *us.*

Reaching for him, my hand came in contact with cold, empty sheets.

Panic gripped me and I sat quickly, looking around my bedroom in the faint light, searching for my mate, afraid he'd changed his mind, gone back to Trion without me. Had he been there at all? Had it been a dream? My body felt well used, my muscles were sore, my pussy ached. I felt his seed in me and knew it hadn't been a dream at all.

It was stupid, I knew. After the way he'd made love to me, held me when the tears came, I had no reason to doubt his devotion to me or to our son.

Still, old habits die hard, and I'd woken many nights over the past year crying and afraid, reliving the nightmare of the attack in my dreams. Imagining him dead, just like the guards who had saved my life in that transport room. Just like the doctor.

Heart racing, I strained to hear him. To hear Noah. Or the damn grandfather clock on the first floor. Anything but cold, empty stillness.

Silence greeted me, and unoccupied space. The door to Noah's room I kept open just a crack, enough for me to hear him crying, but not so much that I heard every breath and wiggle of his precious little body.

The first two or three weeks after I'd brought him home, I'd checked him about every thirty minutes, worried he'd stop breathing. But now, I slept hard and uninterrupted. Four in the morning. He was a good sleeper, but this was generally the time of night Noah woke up hungry, grumpy, and wet.

Where was Roark?

I slid from bed, naked from Roark's loving. He'd carried me here and taken me again, sliding into me from behind, his cock stretching me open as he caressed me with his hands, played with my ringed nipples and my clit, made me come in a whimpering, quivering mess. By the time he was finished with me, I'd fallen asleep in the cocoon of his arms, his chest pressed to my back, his cock deep inside.

I wanted to fall asleep like that every night for the rest of my life.

I pulled my knee-length silk robe on to cover myself and tiptoed to Noah's room. Cracking the door as quietly as possible, my gaze drifted to the crib.

Empty.

Shoving the door open in a rush, I burst into the room, ready to yell for Miranda. I allowed her to help me with

Noah during the day, when I was too tired to care for him. But at night, that precious little baby was all mine.

I hurried toward the crib, my heart lodged in my throat.

"What are you doing, mate?" Roark's low voice stopped me cold.

Whirling, I turned to find him in the rocking chair next to the bay window, our son lying contentedly in his arms, drinking from a bottle. "Roark? What are you doing?"

"Feeding my son." His face was so relaxed, so serene. I'd never seen that expression on his face before. He looked up at me with a soft smile. "You should be asleep, mate. You need rest, and I know my demands on you were too much. Return to bed. Noah is content, as am I. We are learning one another."

I watched, shocked, as Noah's little hands drifted to his father's chin. Roark dipped his head so Noah could grab his nose, his lips, his beard. Noah's eyes were wide open and curious as he drank from the bottle. A second bottle sat in the warmer next to the crib, as he was generally a very hungry little boy.

"He'll drink both bottles," I told him.

"Greedy, are you?" Roark didn't lift his head from his son. They were gazing into each other's eyes in a mutual love-fest that made my heart ache so badly I lifted my hand to my chest and rubbed the area. Tears gathered against my will, slipping silently from my eyes to slide down my cheeks in the darkness.

I used my sleeve to wipe them away and that action caught Roark's attention. "Are you unwell, Natalie?"

"No. I'm perfect." I sniffed then, because the tears were starting to back up and making my nose run.

Roark grinned. "Come here."

I went to them, to my boys, and felt like a kid at Christmas as Roark shifted Noah to the side and made room for me on his lap. I crawled onto him, leaned my head on his chest and listened to his heart beating.

Roark settled Noah half on my lap, half on his chest, his strong arms keeping us both safe and warm.

"I love you, Roark." The words burst from me and I couldn't hold them back. This moment was the best of my entire life. And all of it was due to the man who held me, my matched mate. I'd have to thank Warden Egara when I saw her again.

"You are my heart and soul, Natalie. You and our son. A few days ago, I was a tortured, lost man. You are a miracle. You made me whole again."

Noah finished the bottle in record time, burping like a world-class champion before settling against us and drifting back to sleep. Normally, he wanted both bottles, a few minutes of play, and then, after a couple hours, would finally settle back down for another two or three hours of sleep.

But Roark sang to him, a strange, haunting melody I'd never heard before. The words of the song were about stardust and moonlight, singing birds and sleep. I assumed it was a Trion lullaby, one I would learn.

"When are we going home?" I asked.

Roark stilled and I heard his breath catch. "You are ready to return to Trion?"

Smiling, I lifted my hand to touch Noah's soft cheek as he slept. "Of course. You can't stay here. Don't you run a whole continent or something? Your people need you."

"Your home is beautiful, Natalie. I wasn't sure…"

It was my turn to stiffen. "Sure about what? You don't want us to come home with you?"

"Without question." When I did not respond, Roark continued. "Look at me."

Predawn light filtered into the room. It was still dark, in a shadowy gray, but I could see him well enough to know his eyes had gone dark with an emotion I could not name.

"I will not leave Earth without you, mate. You are mine. Do you understand?"

"Yes." I knew I belonged to him. My body, sore in all the right places, knew it, too.

"But we can take some time, if you prefer. I calculated the time difference as you slept. We can spend weeks here, if that would make you happy and it will only be a day or less on Trion. I left Seton in charge. He is a good and capable leader. We do not need to rush, mate. I want you to be happy, to be ready."

"I'm ready now." Looking around the room, I knew I spoke the truth. Nothing in this house mattered to me. My home was in Roark's arms. I lifted my hand to his cheek and made sure my heart was in my eyes. "I go where you go, Roark. You are my home now."

With a soft groan, he lowered his head to kiss me, our son jostled between us just enough to fidget and squirm. We both ignored him, the gentle heat of the kiss too heady, too intoxicating to hurry.

The door handle rattled and I leaned back, ending the kiss, expecting Miranda to enter the room to check on Noah.

But the man who stood in the entry was dressed head to toe in black, and the weapon in his hand was pointed at the crib, where Noah's sweet body would have been if Roark were not here, holding us.

Before I could react, Roark rose from the chair like a monster in the dark. He turned his back to the intruder, spinning Noah and I away from the door. I stumbled, then instinctively grabbed Noah from him.

I heard gunfire with a silencer, like I'd heard a hundred times in an action movie, but it was louder than I expected and Roark jerked in pain as he was shot in the back.

I wrapped my body around Noah and kept my back to the door as Roark released us both with a bellow of rage. He spun around and rushed the door.

Two more gunshots. One must have hit Roark, for I heard him grunt in pain. The other went wide, a burst of sound to my right as the wall above Noah's crib disintegrated where the bullet hit.

I dropped to my knees and scrambled for the open door to my bedroom. I had a handgun in my bedside drawer, right next to the small dagger Roark had given me, the gold blade that saved my life. Since the attack on Trion, knowing I had weapons nearby was the only way I could sleep at night, alone.

Noah woke and began to cry. Roark bellowed in rage and I heard his huge body crash into the attacker. The sounds of fists and snarls urged me on.

The crib in Noah's room collapsed with a loud snapping sound.

Out of sight, I rose to my feet and ran. When I reached the other side of the bed, I placed my screaming son on the floor and pulled open the drawer. The gun was there, as was the blade. I grabbed both and ran back to the open door just as Roark threw the intruder out into the hallway.

I raised the gun, my hands shaking, but couldn't get a clear shot around Roark's huge frame.

Blood ran down Roark's bare back from at least two gunshot wounds, but he stood tall and strong like a beast among men.

The attacker must have panicked, for he scrambled through the hallway, his footsteps loud as he raced down the curved wooden staircase.

I expected Roark to give chase, but he stood there panting and I could not leave my post, half in, half out of my bedroom. I could not leave Noah unprotected.

"Roark?"

The front door slammed against the wall and I knew the attacker was gone. Across the hall, Miranda opened her door and screamed when she saw Roark.

He staggered then, leaning against the wall.

Miranda rushed past me, saw the destroyed crib and gasped. "Where's Noah? Where's the baby?"

Even though I could hear his angry crying, I said, "He's in my room, on the floor."

"I'll get him." Miranda rushed past me and I sighed in relief as Noah's wails calmed immediately to the sound of her crooning words. She reappeared in the door, Noah safely in her arms.

"Natalie."

I rushed to his side and slid under his arm, helping to hold him upright. He was heavy and I bit my lip as he leaned against me with a lot more weight than I was expecting. God, he was huge.

"Miranda, call 9-1-1. Roark needs an ambulance."

"No, mate. I would not let your hack physicians touch me. Your Earth bullets, fortunately, went through me, so there is no need to retrieve them. Get my bag and use the ReGen Wand. That will heal me enough to get back to Trion and the pod." I dashed into the other room, grabbed the small bag he'd brought with him, pulled out a small metal wand thing. It looked much like the device he'd used on me for his medical exam. Well, the probing. It was more of an orgasm by magical dildo than exam. Running back, I gave it to Roark, who pushed a button. A blue light came on.

"Wave this over my back."

I did as he said and watched as his body healed somewhat, thankful it didn't go someplace private. While Roark was sweating and he breathed raggedly, I could see the tenseness leave his shoulders. The pain was lessening. As Miranda and I watched over the next few minutes, the wounds had closed up mostly, the blood stopping.

"Good. Enough," he said, reaching to grab the wand. "If it gets worse, we'll use it again and again to stave off the worst. We must get back to the brides processing center. Someone on Earth wants to do us harm."

I shook my head. "But that's in Miami!"

"Your parents keep their plane at the municipal airport," Miranda reminded me. "I'll call and have it readied to take us to Miami."

The thought had never occurred to me to use my parents' private plane. Since they were overseas and the plane didn't have that reach, they went first class on commercial flights. Their jet was just waiting to be used.

"Thank you," I said to Miranda. "Tell them we'll be there in twenty minutes."

oark

I COULDN'T WAIT to get off this primitive fucking planet. The ReGen wand was the only thing keeping me well enough to protect my family and see us to the transport center. Money spoke here on Earth, just as it did on Trion. Natalie had not mentioned that she came from wealth. Of course, we'd had one night together and we hadn't done much talking.

The size of her home, the fact that she had servants to assist her, the extravagance of the furnishings and art in her home all led me to believe she was wealthy. But the airplane was something else entirely.

Natalie's jet was small and slow, nothing like the ships used in the Coalition Fleet, but it was the best they had on Earth. I assumed their military had better, faster ships, but had no way to know for sure. Nor did I care. My highest priority was to get my mate and my son home to Xalia where I could surround her with guards, keep her safe and sleep beside her every night. The jet was slow, but I was thankful for it now, knowing I could get Natalie and Noah—and the woman, Miranda, who seemed to be my mate's second—to the brides program's transport center faster than by any other means.

An efficient woman, Miranda had arranged for our transportation within moments. She had driven a large vehicle while Natalie and I sat in the back next to a large seat Noah was buckled into like a warrior's battle harness. Natalie said it was a car seat, but since we, too, sat in seats inside the vehicle, I did not understand the significance. Miranda drove us the short distance to the airstrip while Natalie ran the ReGen wand over my wounds, one after another. As soon as the bleeding stopped in one wound, she would move on to the next. But each time I moved, the wounds would tear open and the blood would flow.

I needed a ReGen pod. I doubted Warden Egara had such technology available to her in the processing center. And I would not allow the primitive human doctors to touch me. They still used steel and primitive stitches to heal major wounds since they were new to the Coalition and did not have access to the more advanced tools of the trade . I did not need to be cut open further. Nor did I wish for a human blood transfusion, as Natalie suggested. I had no doubt my body would reject any such efforts by the human doctors.

No. I needed to get my family off this planet. And quickly. If I didn't get to a ReGen pod, I'd most likely die within a few hours.

I must have blacked out for most of our flight to Miami. When I woke, Warden Egara stood over me. She had two military brutes with her, humans, ready to haul me off the airplane.

They lugged me to my feet, cursed at how big I was, but threw their arms around me and assisted me to the waiting vehicle. Warden Egara was already in the driver's seat. The vehicle was larger than Natalie's and all of us piled into the long black vehicle. Inside were four rows of additional seats. Natalie sat on one and the human men lay me down next to her, my head in her lap. She ran her fingers through my hair as the men applied pressure to my wounds.

"Are you guys EMTs?" Natalie asked the dark-skinned man leaning over my chest. His hair was darker even than mine, a pure black like the deep shadows of space. His skin was a deep brown, his eyes dark pools I could not read. He was pushing down on my shoulder and chest, hard, the pain like a knife blade shoved deep.

"Paramedic," he answered, nodding his head at his friend who leaned over the back of the seat. The second man applied pressure to the wounds in my back. "He's a field medic."

Natalie nodded. "Marines?"

The man behind me had skin a pale, pasty white, with bright auburn hair. They were obviously a different type of human and I wondered at the difference between all of them in awe. Natalie, with her pale hair and fair skin, the warden with her dark hair and darker skin. And these two men, on opposite extremes of color from one another. Once, long ago, Trion had been more colorful, our people more varied. But over the ages we had blended into a single race. Our uniqueness now came from breeding with aliens, like Natalie. People from other planets.

The pale man shook his head and twisted his hand, making me groan in pain. "No. Army. Used to be." He grunted at me. "Sorry, man. But you're bleeding like a stuck pig."

I had no idea what that meant, but it couldn't be good.

"Used to be?" Natalie asked.

Pale man nodded. "Yeah. Used to be. Now we belong to the Interstellar Coalition."

The dark-skinned man smiled. "Sort of. Usually, we handle supply and personnel transport between Earth and the Colony. Today is a bit more exciting."

"What colony?" Miranda piped up from the back as Noah made bubbling, blowing noises. I imagined him with his chubby little hand in his mouth, drooling all over her.

"The contaminated," I answered. Everyone in the Coalition Fleet knew about the planet colonized by Prillon Prime. They sent their warriors there to live out their days if, during the course of battle, they were captured and contaminated by Hive technology. The settlement was originally designed just for Prillon warriors, but as more and more warriors had trouble assimilating into civilian populations with their new cyborg implants, the colony's population swelled to include other races.

"Careful, bro." The dark-eyed man stared down at me and I opened my eyes to discover the telltale silver ring around his iris. He might have been human once, but he was more than human now.

"I meant no offense."

"You fight those bastards?"

"Yes. Four years in Sector 843. I have no love for the Hive." I'd volunteered to serve in the coalition Fleet the morning of my twentieth birthing day. Four years on a battleship fighting the scourge of the universe was more than enough. I'd done my time, and summoned my bride, as was my due.

He stared down at me, sizing me up, until his counterpart broke the tension. "Mostly, we just do whatever Warden Egara tells us to do."

Natalie looked confused but I didn't have the strength to explain. I would answer all of her questions in time.

"They're my guys. You can trust them." Warden Egara tossed the words over her shoulder. I ignored all of them, focused on Natalie's fingers running through my hair and the sound of Miranda cooing to my son in the backseat as thought of space and war and the Hive drifted from my mind. If not for my time in the war, I would not have my mate. With Natalie's loving touch soothing me, I did not regret a single moment of that hell.

The Warden's movements were calm and efficient as she pulled into the parking garage of the brides processing center and I wondered about her history. She was very calm, considering the chaos surrounding her. Still, Natalie trusted her and I could see love in her eyes every time she looked at Noah. That meant I trusted her, too.

The warden's man helped me out of the vehicle and onto an elevator. Once we were all inside, the warden hit a button and the doors slid closed. She turned to me, addressing me for the first time.

"I would say, Councilor Roark, that it is good to see you again, but it seems you have run into some trouble here on Earth."

"An assassin."

She raised her brow but said nothing as the doors slid open and she led us to the transport room. The men settled me in a chair as the warden moved to the control panel. "I need transport codes. This might take a few minutes."

I sat, slumping to my right and into a position I found most comfortable. Natalie moved behind me and waved the wand over my back again, the pain easing slightly. Miranda stood nearby and swayed, rocking Noah as he looked around with wide, curious eyes. He'd eaten and fussed on the airplane, then slept the entire flight. I had to hope he would sleep during transport. The bright light and sensations might scare him.

Warden Egara spoke to the red-haired man who had joined her at the controls. "Trion. Xalia's transport center. Set the coordinates."

"Yes, ma'am. They just sent new codes. Five minutes."

"Tell them to prepare a healing pod. He'll need it as soon as we return," Natalie ordered.

"A ReGeneration pod?" The warden looked to me for confirmation of the extent of my injuries. I nodded.

"Tell Doctor Brax to implement my arrival plan, as previously discussed."

She looked at me strangely, but transmitted exactly what I told her. That done, she looked at me and crossed her arms over her chest, the calm, efficient woman replaced by a furious female. "Tell me about the assassin."

"I was followed to Natalie's home," I said. "Someone knew of my arrival, Natalie's location here on Earth, and the reason for my visit."

She spun about, pacing. "Followed? From here?"

"How else do I explain the attack on my family?"

"Why would someone wish to attack you on Earth?"

"The same reason I was taken and tortured on Trion."

"You think this is somehow connected to the ambush on Trion?" The warden scowled, a thick line appearing between her delicately arched brows. She was actually quite beautiful. "But that's impossible. That would mean there is a Trion spy here, in this facility."

I shrugged, then winced as pain exploded through my chest and back at the simple movement. "Is there another transport center nearby?"

"No. The closest transport center is in Europe."

Natalie gasped. "There's no way he followed you from Europe. He would have been days behind you."

"They came from Miami, Warden. That is the only explanation that makes sense. While it seems like a great amount of time has passed since Natalie returned to Earth, over a year, for me, it has been ten days. Someone wants me, or something from me. Why else would I have been kept alive when the rest of Outpost Two was murdered? Someone followed me."

Warden Egara moved to work the controls besides the man arranging transport. Her hands flew over the flat screen. "Let me check the logs."

Her eyes narrowed as she read. "I have your transport record and communications from yesterday, then a bride who was transported today to Atlan. There is nothing… wait."

Her hand stilled, her eyes widened. Her fingers moved frantically. "An encrypted message was sent an hour after your transport. The center was closed when the message came through. The communication should have been rerouted to the processing center in Paris. They were on call last night."

She turned to look at me, then at Natalie, who still waved the wand behind my back.

"There is one message here. One moment while I decipher it."

I was impressed with her abilities. She was more like a Coalition fighter than an Earth female, then remembered through my sluggish brain our conversation from the day before. She'd been matched and mated to Prillon warriors who had died.

Her body stilled as she scanned the screen. "The message came from Xalia's transport center and it reads: *Councilor Roark's medallion pinged on Earth. Roark is on Earth. Find Earth coordinates for human mate, Natalie Montgomery. Boston. Eliminate both. Bring medallion to me.*"

I felt Natalie's hand still. The pain ceased completely in one spot, as the wand focused on healing one specific area.

"Someone wants the medallion?" she asked.

I looked over my shoulder at her. Her cheeks were pale, her eyes wide. I enjoyed seeing her face flushed with passion and need instead of this haggard concern and confusion. As soon as we were back on Trion, I was healed, and whomever was trying to gain access to my medallion was dead, I was going to fuck her for a week.

"Why do they want this medallion?" Warden Egara asked.

"It is a key to the subterranean vault on Trion for the southern continent. Each councilor holds a key for a vault in their part of the planet."

"What's in the vaults? You mentioned it, but not specifically," Natalie said.

"Weapons. Technology. Wealth. We live a simple life, but that does not mean we aren't prepared for a Hive attack."

Warden Egara harrumphed. "Apparently, someone wants to use the weapons to conquer Trion instead."

"That's my problem. The spy in your program, is yours, Warden."

"A mole," Natalie said, using an Earth term I'd never heard before.

The warden looked grim. "You take care of your problem, Councilor, and I'll take care of mine. He won't live long. Not now that I know I need to hunt him."

"The transport is ready, Warden." The dark-skinned soldier interrupted our conversation. "Councilor, they said to tell you that a Doctor Brax is on standby with Seton and a medical team."

"Excellent." Time to go home. I moved to rise, Natalie helping me.

Miranda handed the baby over to my mate, tears in her eyes her only goodbye. We were going across the universe and never coming back.

"You must come with us," Natalie told Miranda, grabbing

her hand. She turned her head and looked to Warden Egara. "She's coming with us."

"What?" Miranda asked, her eyes wide, shaking her head. "I can't. I'm not matched. I can't go to Trion! It's not like a quick trip to Florida."

"We're not coming back. Please come with us. I'm selfish and I need you."

"She isn't matched," Warden Egara said. "As Councilor of Trion, Roark could grant permission. But you—" she pointed at me, "—can't wait any longer for that pod."

The ReGen wand's effects were waning again. I did need the pod.

"Roark, please."

"It's not up to me. I will do whatever makes you happy, *gara*, but Miranda must choose for herself."

"Come with us," Natalie pleaded. "It's lovely there. We will find you a mate. You have no one here. No family. Take a chance. I did, and look what I have."

Miranda looked scared.

Warden Egara told the woman. "There is no time. You must choose now. I can't allow a Trion Councilor to die on my transport pad."

Miranda nodded fervently. "All right. I'll go."

Natalie grabbed her hand and pulled her toward the transport pad. I ensured we were all together, that the baby was settled in my mate's arms. Through gritted teeth, I thanked the warden.

She nodded once. "Good luck. May you find happiness in the universe. Your transport will begin in three... two... one."

* * *

NATALIE

. . .

137

THE TRANSPORT WAS a blue flash of light like the last time, but I didn't have a murdering madman after me. This time, I wasn't crying because my mate was dead. I wasn't screaming for the doctor and the guards who'd protected me. I had my mate and my son with me. I had Miranda. And the little dagger Roark had given me in the oasis was tucked snuggly into my boot. I wasn't getting near a transport center again without the weapon. Roark didn't need to know my anxiety since he was injured, but I felt better knowing I could keep us all safe if something happened.

We were going back to Trion, to doctors and guards and Roark's people. But we weren't safe yet.

It felt like I drifted in and out of consciousness for hours, holding tightly to Noah where he rested in my arms. I had no idea how much time had passed when the lights and pressure faded. I woke lying on a hard floor, Noah resting on my chest. Miranda appeared to be sleeping a few steps away, and Roark's blood already soaked the pad beneath his back.

I opened my mouth to scream for help, but the med team surrounded Roark at once. I eyed them all, thinking one might be the mole. But they didn't want him. No, not now that it was known I had the medallion. They wanted me.

"Councilor." A man close in age to Roark came to him at once. He was tall, dark and handsome, of course. His pants were black, as was his tunic, but he had some sort of colored insignia on his chest, and the men surrounding him obeyed his commands. "Roark, my friend, you always show up bleeding and half dead. It's not funny anymore."

"Cease your whining, Seton, and see to my mate. There is a traitor among us."

Noah chose that moment to stir in my arms and let out a blood-curdling scream.

Everyone froze in place and turned to look at me. At Noah.

As Roark was settled onto a Trion version of a stretcher, three people waving ReGen wands over him, he spoke. "Natalie and I have discovered that time on Earth passes differently than it does here. How long was I gone, Seton?"

"Thirty-five minutes," Seton replied. "We notified your parents and they transported here to await your return."

Thirty-five minutes? I was seeing now how Roark was so stunned that I'd had a baby when just a few days had passed for him.

"Take care of my mate, Seton. And my son. See to them first."

"Son?" Seton asked, then, "What traitor? Roark, what the *fark* happened to you?"

"I will not say and leave my family vulnerable while I am healing. I want two sets of guards on duty at all times. Have my parents stay with Natalie and Noah. Trust no one."

Seton ushered Roark toward a strange, oblong coffin-looking thing glowing with light. Roark looked at me as they lowered him inside. "Protect Noah, mate. Trust Seton and my parents. No one else."

He held my gaze until I nodded. Noah was tugging at my hair and I absently grabbed his little wrists, holding him in place so I could think without him yanking hair out of my head. "We'll be fine, Roark. Heal. We'll be here when you wake up."

Roark nodded and tore his gaze from mine to look at an older man leaning over the edge of the pod adjusting the controls. "How long this time, Doctor Brax?"

The older gentleman sighed, a wry smile on his face, and I assumed this was not the first time Roark and the doctor had this conversation. "I recommend a full twenty-four hours, Councilor. You weren't fully healed the last time."

Roark grinned back at him. "That's too long. I can't leave my mate unprotected for that long."

I opened my mouth to protest, but Seton beat me to it. "I'll protect her with my life, Roark. I won't leave her side. You have my word."

Roark looked to his friend and I saw the decision there even before he nodded. "She is my life, Seton."

"I know."

Roark nodded and turned to the doctor. "Twenty-four hours and not a minute more."

"Excellent. You are making the right decision, sir." The doctor's hands sped to twice their previous speed and I assumed it was to knock Roark out before my stubborn mate changed his mind. I wasn't eager to have him asleep and away from me for that long, but if it meant he would heal completely, then it would be worth it.

"*Gara.*"

A transparent covering slid into place over Roark's face and he was surrounded by bright light. He was staring at me and I watched as his eyelids fluttered, then closed as he was put under for the healing process.

Once Roark was completely under, everyone in the room turned to look at me. Me and Noah.

Sheesh. Talk about feeling like a bug under a microscope. I was wearing jeans and a T-shirt I'd tugged on before leaving for the airport, covered in Roark's blood from the many times I'd used the ReGen wand to heal him. Miranda cleared her throat behind me and I took a step back, closer to her. I'd completely forgotten she was with me.

I turned to find her staring, her jaw open, as Seton broke the tension and walked straight over to us. I'd been on Trion for two days, not much more than Miranda, but I was not afraid. I was glad to be back.

"You must be Natalie." His voice was deep and gentle, as if he was afraid both of us would bolt.

Miranda looked from him to me. I nodded to her that we

were okay and turned to address Seton. "Yes, I am Natalie. This is Miranda."

He bowed low and went down on one knee before me. Miranda's hand came to rest on my shoulder and Noah stilled in my arms, looking down on the man with curiosity. "I am Seton, my lady. I pledge my honor to you and will protect you and your son with my life."

My jaw went slack as I wondered how to respond. This felt like a formal ritual, and I had no idea what I was supposed to say.

"It's customary, daughter, to accept his offer and give him permission to rise." The voice was female, confident, and coming from just behind me. I turned to find an older female dressed in cream and gold, an older version of Roark standing just behind her looking almost as fierce and imposing as his son.

Licking my lips, I turned back to Seton, who remained on one knee before me, head bowed. "Thank you, Seton. I accept and, umm, you may rise now."

Seton rose to stand before me, towering over Miranda and I both, just like Roark did. But I didn't focus on him now. He was a known. He was Roark's friend, the one man my mate said I could trust on this planet. Having him at my back made me feel confident enough to face the older couple—my in-laws—who may or may not want an alien daughter-in-law.

"My son?" she said to Seton as she peeked into the pod at Roark.

As if she didn't need to say more, Seton explained the injuries and the duration of his stay in the pod.

"We have been briefed on what happened, although we will get more details from you. Later."

I could only nod, pleased to know she was concerned for her son's welfare and interested in learning the reasons for his wounds.

I turned, Noah in my arms, and found Roark's father smiling broadly. He stood just behind his wife, clearly at ease with the situation. While he glanced at the pod that held his healing son, he looked to me kindly. Roark's mother, however, had her arms crossed and scrutinized me from head to toe as if sizing me up, or deciding whether or not I passed inspection.

Yes, she was my mother-in-law. Cue the horror film music.

She stepped forward, her gaze never leaving mine. I held my chin up and refused to look away. I was not going to be cowed by some fifty-year-old alien woman, even if she was my mother-in-law. No. *Especially* because she was my mother-in-law. Show weakness now and she'd run roughshod over me for the rest of my life. I'd heard all the horror stories and seen all the movies. I knew the score.

"You must be Roark's mother."

"I am Tracen. Roark is my son." Her gaze drifted lower, settled on Noah briefly, then returned to my face. "You must be Natalie, Roark's matched mate."

"Yes." I had no idea where this was going. Roark had told me his mother suggested the brides program because he needed a mate, to breed her. From what I remember, he'd said he'd agreed and found the perfect match. Me. But that didn't mean Roark's parents approved of an Earth woman for their son. I didn't know if they would want their grandson, a child who was half-alien. My own mother hadn't wanted anything to do with Noah, so I didn't expect what happened next.

Roark's mother stepped forward and wrapped me in her arms. She sobbed, squeezing Noah and I both so tightly my son started to fuss.

"Welcome, my daughter. The gods have blessed us this

day with a new daughter and a grandson. You brought Roark back to us, Natalie of Earth. I can never repay you for this miracle. Welcome. Welcome to our family." Her voice cracked on the last, her cheek pressed to mine where I felt the wet trail of her tears.

I stood there, stiff, my arms wrapped around Noah as she hugged us both and cried. It was awkward and I glanced at the sleeping Roark in the pod, wishing he were awake to help me.

Roark's huge father stepped forward and wrapped his arms around his mate, me, and Noah, and I immediately felt safe and protected. "Welcome, daughter." His deep rumble was so similar to Roark's that even little Noah stilled.

"I— Thank you." I had no idea what to say, or how to react. This was *not* what I expected. First, Seton kneeling like I was some kind of princess, and now this.

Had they let me go, I would have been fine. But they did not release me, not for long minutes, as if they needed to drink us in, their new daughter and precious grandchild. Their love was palpable. I assumed it was love. I'd never felt such drowning emotion from my own parents. Not once. Not as a child coming home for summer break, high school graduation, college graduation, when I gave birth. Never.

This was what I'd been missing.

I cracked, and tears tracked my own cheeks as they continued to hold me in the shelter of their arms. "Roark is a lucky man, to have parents like you."

Tracen chuckled and finally pulled back. "Not to hear him grumble." Her smile was genuine and full of teasing. Shell-shocked, I stood still as her gaze lowered to Noah and her smile went from warm to raw, barefaced love. "He looks just like his father." Her gaze darted to me, then back to Noah. "But he has your eyes."

Holding Noah in my arms brought me great comfort, knowing he was safe. "Yes. His name is Noah."

Noah squirmed and Roark's parents stepped back, both of them looking at him like the doting grandparents I'd dreamed he could have.

"May I hold him?" Tracen asked.

I smiled. God, I was so fucking easy. One real hug and she'd completely won me over. Just that fast, I was willing to hand over my child. "Of course, but he's going to be hungry soon."

Tracen held out her arms and I settled Noah there before turning to Miranda. "Did we transport with the diaper bag?"

"Of course. But not enough to last forever." Miranda looked at Tracen, then at me, apprehensive. "I... I don't know what anyone is saying."

I stared at Miranda, not realizing why.

"Why doesn't she have an NPU?" Roark's father asked.

Oh, hell. I'd forgotten all about that stupid needle thing, and the neuroprocessor that Warden Egara gave me to understand their language. "We were rushed by Roark's injuries. She didn't have time to get one."

"We will have that taken care of right now. Poor thing, she must be so lost." Roark's father turned to the doctor. "Doctor Brax, this woman needs an NPU immediately."

I'd forgotten all about the translator thing. When I'd had mine inserted, I'd just finished that flaming-hot testing dream. Miranda had been dragged ten light years, to an alien world, and couldn't understand a word anyone but me was saying. "Sorry, Miranda. They're going to give you one of their translators so you can understand everyone."

"If Miranda will sit in one of the exam chairs, she can have that done right now. Please reassure her it doesn't hurt and... well, you've had it done."

"Thank you... um, I don't know what to call you," I said to

Roark's father as I took Miranda's hand and led her to the chair Doctor Brax indicated.

"Aran."

I nodded in reply, then explained everything to Miranda. I stood and held her hand as she had the NPU inserted in the bone of her temple, just behind her ear.

Noah began to fuss in Tracen's arms. "He's probably hungry."

"Yes," Tracen replied. "I'm surprised he's not asleep. All of you. The first time you transported, you slept when we came to meet you."

"I did?" I wasn't even aware of their visit.

"Yes, our son is very possessive. I can see why."

"Better?" I asked Miranda, once she started to look around wide-eyed, understanding everyone in the med unit.

She smiled now, much more at ease. "Wow. It's amazing. Thank you." When the baby fussed again, she said, "Do you have infant formula here? Natalie does her best to feed him, but he's a hungry little monster and her body just can't keep up."

Tracen was cooing and nuzzling her grandson, and didn't bother lifting her head as she answered. "I do not know what infant formula is, but I've raised two children. We will make sure you have everything you need."

My shoulders sagged. Was it really going to be this easy? I couldn't believe it. Roark would be completely healed by this time tomorrow, and I'd finally have the family I'd always dreamed of.

Roark's father turned to Miranda. "I am surprised you accompanied Natalie on such a great journey."

I had no idea what the protocols would be, but I wanted her protected, so I interrupted before Miranda could respond. "She's my friend and Noah loves her. I couldn't leave her behind."

"Of course not." Tracen smiled and hugged Miranda with one arm, Noah in the other. Noah squealed with excitement, his hunger temporarily forgotten, as he focused on Miranda's face. He truly did love her, as she'd helped me care for him from the day we brought him home from the hospital. "Welcome to the family, Miranda. You belong to us now, and we will protect you as we do Natalie and Noah."

Miranda blinked slowly, letting everything sink in, especially now that she understood. I smiled at her like I had a thousand times before, like sisters, and she smiled back. "Thank you."

Tracen let her go, but Noah screeched and reached his chubby little arms for the familiar comfort of Miranda's arms.

Reluctantly, Tracen let him go.

"He just doesn't know you yet," I hurried to reassure her.

"Oh, I know, dear. Don't worry. That won't be the case for long."

Behind her, Roark's father chuckled, pulling his mate backward and wrapping his arms around her. "He will love you, *gara*, as your son and I do."

She turned to look up at her mate and the love I saw shining between them made my heart skip a beat. So much love, after so many years. My parents had never looked at each other the way these two aliens did. Not once.

Seton cleared his throat behind me, where I'd completely forgotten him. "My apologies, my lady, but we should get you to a more secure location for the night. All of you."

I turned to look at him, but was immediately distracted by the sight of Roark's unconscious form inside the pod thing. "I want to stay with him." I couldn't leave his side. Not again. Especially since the bad guys—what else was there to call them?—wanted the medallion and I had it. With Miranda here, and Roark's parents, I knew Noah would be safe and protected. Roark, however, was alone. I didn't want him to be alone. I wanted my face to be the first thing he saw when he awoke.

Turning to Miranda, I was prepared to plead, but she was already shaking her head. "No problem, Natalie. I can handle Noah for one night. Stay with Roark. He needs you."

Seton stepped forward on my left. "He is unconscious, my lady. He will not even know you are here. You should rest."

I opened my mouth to protest, but my gaze met Tracen's before I could form the words I needed to argue.

"Let her stay, Seton. He'll know she's here. Trust me. He'll know. The guards can escort her should she wish to come to Noah at any time."

Seton crossed his arms, one eyebrow raised, and looked to Roark's father, who shrugged. "Don't look at me, Seton. They are matched. And our females are stubborn. You can't win this argument." He looked at his son in the pod, his eyes clouding with anger. "Unless you are worried for her safety here. Can you protect her? Roark will have both our heads if anything happens to his mate."

Seton unfolded his arms. "Yes. I have more than enough guards to protect two locations. But Miranda and Noah will need to stay with you. I do not have enough men I trust to guard three locations."

"Of course, she'll come with us." Tracen slipped from her mate's arms and went to Miranda's side, wrapping her hands around the younger woman's arm. "Come with us, dear. The guest room at our house has a nice, soft bed, and we'll get Noah fed and settled. Then you can get some rest. How you are still awake after transport I have no idea."

I stepped forward and kissed Noah's soft, downy head before waving Miranda and my new in-laws away. Seton stayed by my side, nodding to a group of guards who saluted and followed my new family out of the medical unit and into a hallway. I had no idea what time it was, but I was exhausted, just as Tracen had said. First, Roark had kept me up half the night making love, then I'd woken before dawn, the attack, the panic, the rush to Miami. And the transport halfway across the galaxy.

I deserved to be tired, right?

Maybe they had one of those pods for exhausted new mothers?

"May I have a chair or something?" I asked Seton.

"Of course." He hurried to the side of the room and brought a chair to me where I stood next to Roark's unconscious form. We were not in a sandy tent, more like a surgical suite in a major hospital. The floors were something like concrete, the walls stone. Everything was sterile and solidly built. "Where are we?"

"Xalia City," Seton answered. "This is the capital of the southern continent, and where Councilor Roark keeps his permanent home."

Whatever. We weren't in the desert, and that worked for me. I had to assume Xalia was a large city, or at least a city with walls.

"Thank you." I sat in the strange sling-style chair. It looked like it folded up for easy transport, but it was soft and comfortable. I curled my legs up underneath me, reassured by the heavy weight of the dagger tucked into my boot, and laid my head on my arms, watching my mate, willing him to know I was here.

"I'm here, Roark. I won't leave your side."

Seton paced behind me. The doctor was working on something on a panel a few steps away. I assumed he was monitoring Roark's healing process, but had no idea what he was truly doing. At the room's entrance, two guards stood at attention. Everyone else was gone.

I turned to look up Seton. "Two guards? Are there more outside?"

"Yes. Do not worry, my lady. I have a full dozen guards surrounding the transport station, and another dozen with your son. Commander Loris is in charge of protecting the station and he is a trusted and well-trained officer."

I didn't care who was in charge. And twelve didn't feel like enough, not after what I'd been through the last time I was on this planet. To him, it had only been ten days, but to me, it felt like a lifetime had passed. "Are there Drovers nearby?"

"No. We are not at Outpost Two. You are in the north, my lady, in a large city. The nearest Drover territory is hundreds of miles from here. You are safe."

Hundreds of miles sounded good, but I wished it were thousands. Millions. But I'd been ten light years away and danger still found me.

"Okay." I returned my attention to Roark.

"Are you hungry?" Seton asked.

To my surprise, my stomach lurched at his question. I was starving. "Yes. Thank you."

Seton bowed and ordered a guard to bring me something to eat. I ate quickly, the warm stew mild but filling. The vegetables were odd, but tasty, and I finished two bowls and a chunk of bread in record time. Stomach full, Roark safe, my eyelids began to drift closed and my head dipped, falling as I slipped into slumber repeatedly.

"My lady." Seton's soft voice didn't fool me. He was going to order me to go lie down somewhere and rest.

"No. I won't leave him."

Seton sighed, and I lifted my arms to the side of Roark's pod, rested my head on my arms and promptly fell asleep in my chair.

CHAPTER 14

 atalie

INTERPLANETARY TRANSPORT GAVE a whole new meaning to "jet lag". My head felt heavy and cloudy as I fought my way out of slumber. The chair I sat in was pressed to the side of Roark's healing pod, and I lifted my head quickly to make sure he was still all right, still healing. But the transparent screen must have had another layer because I couldn't see him anymore. The window into the pod was covered in a thick black screen. I couldn't even tell if he was still in there. The machine still hummed beneath my arms though.

I leaned back and tried to look at the controls I'd seen the doctor using earlier. They looked all right, but I had no idea what any of it meant. It wasn't like on Earth, with a heartbeat monitor and a blood pressure reading up in one corner, beeping to indicate some change. This was so far past advanced, I was lost. Their symbols were strange and I didn't understand any of it. And, I realized, I had no idea about

Trion physiology anyway. What was normal for a human might not be normal for them.

Fortunately, Noah was a healthy baby, no reasons to visit a doctor other than a simple well check. No one had questioned the possibility of him being half Trion. Of course, he had been the only half-alien baby on Earth. It wasn't like the doctors asked, and I never volunteered the information.

With nothing better to do, I shifted and leaned back, bracing my bent elbow on the arm of the chair. I settled my chin in my hand and took a deep breath. I wondered if Noah was all right, if he was awake and cranky. Hungry.

A heavy stillness seemed to have settled in the air and I recognized the quiet. Many times I'd been up in the middle of the night, when the rest of the world slept, to care for my son. There was a certain peaceful solitude that almost soaked the very air with quiet attention. Seton told me we were in a city, but I felt like a solitary figure alone in the night.

Soft snoring came from my left and I turned to find Seton lying on the floor not far from me, asleep. He'd rolled out a basic blanket of some sort, and now slept. I turned to the closed door, a sliver of dread making its way down my back like a drop of icy water sliding over my skin. No one else was in the room. No doctors, no technicians. The door was closed, but no guards stood at attention.

Where were the guards?

I uncurled from the chair, placing my feet on the floor just as the door slid open on silent hinges. I recognized Commander Loris from earlier and I sighed in relief.

"Commander. Thank you. I was worried when I didn't see the guards," I murmured, trying to keep my voice low.

He closed the door quietly behind him and turned to study Seton's sleeping form. "My lady, I'm sorry if I startled you. It appears Seton is a victim of the long day."

"Yes." I smiled. "He's very loyal to Roark."

He nodded. "Yes, he is." Taking a step forward, he approached the healing pod. "How is the councilor doing in there?"

I turned away from him with a shrug. "I have no idea. I don't know how to read the control panel and the doctor isn't here."

The commander tucked his arms behind his back and strolled around to the edge of the room, leaning to the side to look behind a partition where the doctor and other medical staff had frequently disappeared and reappeared earlier. "Ah, yes. Doctor Brax. He is there, on his cot, sound asleep as well."

"Well, it is the middle of the night." It did seem odd though. Even on Earth, there was at least one nurse awake, even in the middle of the night.

"Yes." He walked back toward me. "And why are you awake, my lady? Did you not eat the stew?"

"Yes, I had two bowls—" My voice trailed off as his words sank in. Why would it matter whether or not I ate the stew? How did he even know I had stew?

"Ah, strange Earth physiology. Hadn't counted on that." The commander walked to the control panel of Roark's pod and started pushing buttons.

"What are you doing?"

"Nothing for you to worry about."

I didn't believe him and unease prickled my skin. "Stop it."

He ignored me and the pod powered down, the lights faded, the low humming ceased. I expected the top to slide open, but nothing happened. It was like the pod was dead, as if he'd pulled the plug. "What are you doing?"

Commander Loris pulled a gun of some kind from his pocket and pointed it at me. "Give me the medallion."

I felt my eyes widen and I took an instinctive step back. "I don't know what you're talking about. Turn the pod back on."

He rushed me, pulling my shirt free of my jeans, his grubby hand reaching up beneath my shirt to look for the chain that would have been dangling low over my stomach had I not tucked the gold links up into my bra.

His look was wild and angry when he didn't find it. "Where is it?"

I shrank back, his stubby fingers repulsive against my skin. I was thankful for his lack of knowledge about Earth underwear. Clearly, he'd never encountered a woman in a bra before. "Get your hands off me."

"Give me the medallion." He was the one that wanted it? He was the one that sent the encrypted message to Earth? He was the one that had tried to have me killed? Have Noah and Roark killed, too?

"Turn the pod back on!" I shouted. Could Roark die inside? Was he trapped? Was he going to suffocate in there?

Commander Loris lifted his hand to my hair and yanked my head back with cruel fingers. Tears welled up in my eyes at the sharp pain and he shoved the weapon right up under my chin. Hard. It didn't look like an Earth gun, but a gun was a gun when it was pressed against your head. "You can give it to me, or I can kill you and take it off your corpse."

"You're insane. You can't use it anyway."

"Oh, I know. But you solved that problem for me." His hot breath fanned my face and I cringed.

"What?"

"Your son, Natalie. At this very moment, my friends are making sure we have him." He lowered his head until his lips hovered over mine in a revolting corruption of a kiss. "Don't worry. I'll be a good daddy. He won't even remember you."

What? Him touch Noah? Never. It was one thing to try to kill me, but no one messed with a mother. Fuck him. I'd gotten the family I'd always wanted. A mate who found me light years across the universe. A son made from our love. Even in-laws who were loving and kind. This asshole wanted to ruin all that? Not a chance in hell.

I lifted my leg and reached into my sock, grabbing the small dagger with my right hand. I came up swinging, aiming for his throat.

I managed to cut under his chin, to slice his jaw to the bone as blood poured down his neck. I'd hurt him, but it wasn't a killing blow.

With a shout, he shoved me forward, over the pod, his hand still in my hair. He slammed the hand holding the knife into the side of the pod over and over until I couldn't maintain my grip. I screamed at the pain, the ruthlessness of his actions. My wrist was broken, and several bones in my hand. I felt—and heard—them snap like twigs and the gold dagger clattered to the floor by my foot.

"Let her go, Loris. It's over." I froze. Roark's voice? What? The commander was holding me against the pod. Roark was still trapped inside. Then how?

"Roark." Commander Loris pressed the end of his gun to my temple and pulled me up off the pod until my back was to his chest, a hostage. The blood seeped down his neck and into his shirt. I could feel it hot and sticky on my shirt from when he'd loomed over me and it dripped.

"Put down your weapon, Councilor, or your mate is dead."

In my periphery, I saw Roark. He was holding a gun similar to the commander's. Every line in Roark's body was tense. Rigid. He lowered the weapon to the floor and stood, his hands in the air. "Let her go."

"Give me the medallion and I'll let her live."

"Let her go, Loris. You can't win. The moment I give you

the medallion, the vault codes will be updated. We'd deactivate the current codes before you could use them."

The commander laughed in my ear, the spittle from his mouth landing on the side of my cheek in a sick wet dollop that almost made me gag. "Not if you're all dead. All but the baby."

I watched the horror of Loris's statement spread across Roark's face, sink into his mind. All of his family, murdered tonight, except his son. My son. The boy kept alive so this insane freak could use his DNA as the medallion's key. And for what? What purpose was all this hatred, all this evil?

I had no idea, but I no longer wanted the damn thing dangling between my breasts. It was more trouble than it was worth. If it was going to represent cruelty and ruthlessness, I didn't want it mixed so intimately with the bond Roark and I shared.

Commander Loris kept one hand to my temple. The other, he plunged down the collar of my shirt, looking for the chain. I twisted in his grip, the touch of his hands repulsive. "No!"

"Let her go," Roark repeated. "Take me."

Loris groped me and laughed when Roark's eyes darkened with fury. "I don't want you. If I were going to keep one of you alive, it'd be her. Breasts like these, with the key to the planet between them?" He grinned viciously.

Asshole.

I lowered my head and bit his wrist like a wild animal, trying not to gag at the flavor of his skin, the dark metallic taste of his blood as it filled my mouth.

With a screech, he yelled and pulled his hand back.

I kicked the gold dagger so it slid across the floor to Roark and yelled his name. I dropped to my knees to give him a clear shot.

Roark yelled, knelt, grabbed the knife, and threw it so

quickly I couldn't track his actions. The dagger imbedded in Loris's right eye socket with a disgusting, thunking sound I never wanted to hear again. Turning my head, I looked away. Bile filled my mouth and I swallowed it down.

The commander toppled and I crawled away from his body, awkwardly and quickly, toward Roark, toward my mate. "Why aren't you in the pod? I don't understand."

My heart was beating so hard I worried it would come out of my chest. My breathing was as ragged as if I had just run a marathon, not taken down a space-gun-wielding crazy man.

Roark pulled me into his arms, inspecting me for injury. His hands and gaze raking over me. "*Fark*, your wrist."

I shook my head, but held it carefully to my chest. "It hurts like a bitch, but I just need the ReGen wand. But, you. You! Explain to me what is going on. You're supposed to be in that damn pod!"

Roark tucked me to his side and picked up the gun he'd dropped moments ago. "I knew the traitor would make his move before I woke from the pod. The doctor, Seton and I agreed prior to my transport to Earth that, upon my return, we would use the pod to lure the traitor out into the open. The wounds I received on Earth weren't part of the plan, but I was healed in a couple of hours. The doctor released me, as agreed, and we set the trap."

I was shaking. Adrenaline was great and all, but the after-effects were a bitch.

"Noah. He said they were going after Noah." I struggled to break free of his arms, but he hushed me, holding me tighter.

I fought him, but he spoke. "Noah is safe, my love. I swear it." He stroked my back, tried to soothe me. "My parents did not take him, or Miranda, to their home. They used a decoy to lure the commander's friends to invade. But my father had a dozen men waiting to capture them. They are all in detention cells deep beneath the city awaiting interrogation. Noah is safe."

I looked over at the commander, dead, the gold dagger protruding from his face, blood dripping onto the sterile floor of the medical facility. I cringed, turned my face into Roark's chest. I could hear his heart beating, steady and even. "Why didn't you tell me?"

"I'm sorry, love. I needed your reactions to be real, sincere."

"But he got in. He could have killed us both."

"I underestimated him, mate, and for that I'm sorry. I did not wish to put *you* in harm's way, only me."

"What?" I said, trying to move off his lap, angry. How dare he put himself in danger?

"We needed to find the traitor so we didn't have to worry, to fear for our safety. I had to eliminate the threat so I could focus on being with you and Noah. I did not count on him lacing the meal with a sedative. It was very clever." He lifted a hand to my cheek, cupping my face. "But not clever enough, for it did not work on you."

No, it hadn't. I ate like a stupid pig and it had barely knocked me out.

"Strange Earth physiology." I quoted a dead man, and grinned as I did it. I must be losing my mind. All humor faded as I stared into my mate's eyes. "Don't ever do that to me again. I can still taste his blood." I'd bitten the commander, torn the flesh from his hand, and the taste of him lingered like ashes in my mouth.

"No. No. No. That won't do at all." Roark's eyes blazed and he pulled me to him, claiming my mouth in a kiss meant to wipe away the taste of danger and fear. I wrapped my uninjured arm around him, ignoring the flood of soldiers that stormed the room.

Roark lifted his head, checked with the guards about the safety of the rest of our family. When one communicated with the guards watching over Noah and Roark's parents, and we learned that everyone was indeed safe, I slumped in Roark's arms and he took that moment of weakness to kiss me again. I gave over to the kiss, needing the love and reassurance I felt in it. I didn't care about the guards in the room. My son was safe. I was safe. And Roark was kissing me, loving me, reminding me what home felt like.

Behind us, someone cleared his throat. I turned to find Seton sitting on the floor as one of the soldiers ran a ReGen wand over him. "You two all right?"

He looked like he'd just woken up from a wild night of partying and drinking, all ruffled and messy, like he'd just gotten out of bed. He was handsome. Perhaps I could set him up with Miranda...

"Give me that damn wand," Roark snarled, grabbing it hastily from the man's fingers and waving it over my wrist. Amazingly, I could feel the bones knitting, healing. His head was lowered to tend to the task, but then his gaze lifted and met mine, watching me until it was completely healed.

"Better?" he asked and I nodded. God, I loved space technology.

Once satisfied I was whole again, Roark tucked me under his chin. "The traitor is dead."

"I can see that." Seton shoved at the medical officer who'd come in with a number of others now that the traitor had been uncovered. She was waving a wand of her own over him. He forced her to stop her ministrations, frustrated probably more by the fact that he'd been drugged than by her attentions, and I hid a grin. These Trion guys all thought they were super-human. Not unlike a lot of alpha cavemen on Earth.

158

But once again, my smile faded. "He's dead, but what about the man who attacked us on Earth?"

Roark's arms came around me and he nuzzled the top of my head. "We don't know, mate. But Warden Egara is on her guard. She knows to watch for any more encrypted messages, to remain vigilant. We've done all we can do from here. We will interrogate the men we captured tonight and hope we discover his identity, although I doubt they will know anything. Earth is very far away, another planet."

"But someone must know," I countered.

"Yes. Warden Egara is an intelligent and formidable opponent. She will discover the truth."

I nodded and tore my gaze from the commander's corpse. Looking at the soldier nearest him, I cleared my throat. "That gold dagger is mine. I want it back."

"Yes, my lady."

Roark looked down at me. "I'll give you a new one, mate. Leave that one be."

I shook my head. "No way. That's the one you gave me. That is the one that saved my life, twice now. I want it back. Cleaned, of course. I might never go anywhere without it, ever again."

"Then you shall have it." He looked to the soldier. "Remove it, once we are gone. Clean the blade thoroughly and return it to my lady first thing in the morning."

"Yes, Councilor."

Roark tugged me up to tuck me into his hold. After nodding to Seton, who was finally letting the woman heal him with the wand, Roark led me from the room, and I let him, eager to be away from the tension and blood. To leave it all behind. "Where are we going?"

"Home."

CHAPTER 15

I HELD Natalie in my arms as we gazed down on our sleeping son. My parents and Miranda were safe below, surrounded by two dozen guards. Commander Loris' men were locked away, awaiting judgment. I would deal with them later, much later. Right now, I needed to stand silent in the peace and safety of my home, our home, and hold my mate.

Traveling from outpost to outpost the last few months had taken its toll on my body and my spirit. Home wasn't a physical place. It was the people you loved. Seeing Noah asleep, his arms bent with his hands up by his ears, soothed my soul in a way I'd never expected.

This moment, with Natalie safe in my arms, looking down at the child we'd made, was a gift I would never take for granted. My mother would be pleased. My wanderlust was gone. There was nowhere on this planet, or any other, I wanted to be other than in my own home with my mate and son safely under my care.

It was time to settle in Xalia, to allow Natalie and Noah to know my parents, to become close. Noah deserved to know his grandparents, to be smothered by my mother's adoration and taught about the world by my father. There would be no more outposts for any of us. If the tribal leaders wanted to see me, from now on, they could make the trek to Xalia or meet with one of my commanders in the field.

Natalie pulled away from me to reach down and stroke Noah's perfect cheek with her hand. "He's so beautiful. He looks like you." She whispered the words into the quiet, careful not to disturb him. Her hand froze and she shook her head, her voice clogging with tears. "I have blood on my hands, Roark. Look at me. I shouldn't touch him. Not like this."

"Come, mate. Our son is safe and protected. Let me take care of you."

I led her to the adjoining rooms and directly to the bathing chamber, stripped her bare. I walked around her, studied every inch of her skin, ensuring the doctor had been thorough, that her wrist was truly healed. I would allow no bruising to remain on her body, no pain. Seeing nothing but lingering blood, I stepped into the shower and pulled her under the warm spray. Using soap and gentle hands to wash away every bit of Loris' blood, I was gentle, massaging sore muscles, worshiping her.

My hands were on her breasts, cupping and stroking them, tugging gently on the chain that hung between them, my mark on her, my claim. The gold sparkled in the light and made her look like some kind of mythical goddess, a creature no mere mortal could claim. I looked into her eyes, saw no remnants of her brush with death, nothing but humor and a hint of arousal.

When the events of the day were washed down the drain, my hands changed from clinical cleaning to soothing, heating touch. I wanted to erase the evil from her body and from her mind.

I felt Natalie's laugh beneath my hands more than heard it. "I think I'm clean there."

"Yes, I think you are," I murmured, my hands sliding lower. "And here? Is your pussy clean as well?"

Had she pulled away, I would have been content to hold her, but she grabbed my wrist and directed my hand to her wet core. "I don't know, mate. I think it might be dirty. You'd better check."

All too eager, I backed her up against the wall of the shower and lowered my lips to her cheek as I slid one finger into her wet pussy. The heat of her body wrapped around my finger like a hot glove and I couldn't help but remember what that felt like around my cock. "It's dripping wet. I guess you are a dirty girl."

"You like it when I'm dirty," she countered.

I did, and the way my cock pulsed and swelled, it liked it, too.

"I know what you like, what you need, what makes you scream."

Her pupils dilated and I knew she was turned on by my words. I didn't need the little gush of arousal onto my fingers to tell me that.

"Tonight, you'll give me everything, *gara*. Your body, your mind. Your submission. Perhaps another baby. Yes?"

She licked her lips, nodded.

"I need to hear you say it."

"Yes."

"That isn't enough," I countered.

She looked confused for a moment, then remembered. It

hadn't even been two weeks for me since she said it last, but for her, it had been much longer.

"*Master.*"

Fark. I groaned and claimed her mouth, fucking her with my finger, slipping a second inside her just so I could hear the little catch in her breath. That one word on her lips made me insane. Powerful. Dominant. I needed to be in control of her, to know she was with me, under me. Safe. Mine. And yet she had all the power, the ability to take me to my knees.

And so I broke the kiss and went willingly, lowered myself until I knelt before her on the stone tile, slid my hands down her body to her thighs and nudged them apart.

I could see her perfect pussy, and my mouth watered to taste it, to burn her essence on my tongue. In my mind.

Putting my mouth on her, I licked her from dripping entrance to swollen clit. Once. Twice. Her body wilted and she leaned back against the shower wall. With my hands on her hips, I held her up as I took her with my mouth. I wasn't gentle.

If I was going to be on my knees before her, I would be ruthless, show her that she was still mine, that her body responded to me. She was sweet and tangy on my tongue, the scent of her so feminine and perfect. My cock pulsed and wept with the need to be deep inside her.

"Come for me, Natalie, and then we'll play."

I didn't give her a chance to think as I slid a third finger into her pussy and sucked her clit into my mouth, flicked the sensitive nub with my tongue over and over as my fingers filled her. Fucked her.

I'd nearly lost her today and that knowledge burned through me as I pressed a little harder, readied her tight pussy for my cock. She was so perfect, so beautiful and ripe. She consumed me and I pushed aside everything but this moment, her body and her surrender.

I could not be gentle. Why should I? My touch, my words were demands. She would submit. She would give me everything. I needed everything.

"Come now." I pulled the orgasm from her. She cried out, the sound of it echoing in the shower, her hands tangling in my hair, fierce and tight, as her pussy clenched and spasmed around my fingers.

The medallion, the key to the vault hung low, just above her abdomen where my son had grown and her body curved with a softness I ached to touch, ached to fill with a baby once again. But I could no longer look at the medallion as a gift to her. It had become a curse, had placed her in danger.

Standing, I lifted the medallion gently, holding it in the palm of my hand. "I will remove this, mate."

Her hand wrapped around my wrist and she stilled. Her chest rose and fell rapidly from her release, but the pleasure faded from her blue eyes. "What?"

Shaking my head, I lowered my forehead until it touched hers. "I will remove it. I'm sorry. I'm so sorry, *gara*."

I kissed her softly, gently, regret in every cell of my body. I'd placed her in danger for my own selfish whim, my desire to follow tradition, to mark her, to make sure every fucking idiot male on this planet knew she was mine.

But being mine placed her at risk. The gold that adorned her made her a target, and that was no longer acceptable. I kissed her, over and over. "I'm sorry. Never again, *gara*."

Her body stiffened, her lips no longer soft and pliant beneath mine, but hard and defiant until, finally, she turned her head away. Her grip on my wrist tightened and her hand shook. "Why? You don't want me anymore? You don't want to mark me? Are you sending us back?"

"Back?"

"To Earth." She looked at me, tears gathering in her eyes,

and behind those tears, hurt and rage. "I won't leave Noah. You can't have him. I'll die before I leave my son."

Confusion froze me in place. Hot water poured over us both as her words seeped through the haze of desire clouding my brain. "Natalie, you are mine. You are not going anywhere. I forbid you to leave my side."

Her chin lifted and she looked up at me with defiance in every line of her body. "You told me this chain, this *adornment*, was how Trion men marked their mates. This was your claim, that it would protect me from claims by other men."

"It is tradition." I rolled the gold chain loosely between my fingers. I would not place her in danger for my own selfish ends. I could stare at my emblem hanging from her perfect nipples for hours, but my pleasure faded when I thought of Commander Loris, and the others in the holding cells, the men who had allies, friends who would continue to target my mate. "I will remove this curse from your body."

"No."

Her refusal stopped me cold and I lifted my head to meet her gaze. "You do not give me orders, mate."

She stepped forward, pushing her body into mine, driving me to the edge of my control when I needed it most. "No. You can't have it back. It's mine."

I turned off the water and carried her to the bedroom. There, where I'd ordered it placed the day I'd submitted to the Interstellar Brides Program's testing, was the traditional claiming bench, warm and ready before the fire.

I carried her to stand beside the bench and set her on her feet before me, kissing her over and over as she stood stiff in my arms, her naked body pressed to mine. My cock wept with pre-cum where it was locked between us as I trailed kisses along her jaw and shoulder.

"I claimed you at the Mirana oasis, but never properly, as is custom on Trion."

"Apparently, you don't plan on claiming me at all."

My growl was pure male instinct at her sass. She was pushing me, testing me. The logical part of my mind recognized the need behind her challenge. I had failed her as a master, as a mate. I had not conquered her, convinced her that I was strong enough to protect her and our son. No, I'd left her for over a year, been injured and then nearly lost her again upon our return to Trion.

Instinct and logic warred within my body until my chest felt as if it would tear in two. My mate had been through much, had suffered much. Logic told me to go gently, to soothe and comfort her, but instinct roared through me like a wild beast, demanding I restrain her, spread her open and tie her to the bench as I should have that first night, fuck her senseless, fuck her until she screamed my name and nothing else.

My cock jumped at the idea and I lifted my hand to her cheek, stared into the fiery defiance in her eyes. Gods, she was beautiful when she raged, my strong, rebellious mate. From this moment on, she was mine to protect, mine to master. *Mine.*

Sinking my hands into her hair, I gripped the base of her neck and held her in place for my kiss. My lips were soft, gentle, the last touch of patience I contained in the kiss. Her lips were hard beneath my softness, unyielding and angry.

"You are mine, mate. And I warned you about defying your master."

"You're not my master. Not anymore." Her breath came in hard pants against my lips. "You don't want me, fine. Let me go. I'll cut the damn chain off myself with a pair of wire cutters when I get home."

"You are home." Holding her still, I kissed her hard, thrust my tongue into her mouth, forced her to yield. With a whimper, she let me in and I claimed her mouth as my own, left her no room to retreat, nowhere to hide from me.

Done with the kiss, I lifted my head, still holding her exactly where I needed her to be. "You're mine, Natalie." I spun her around to face the bench, pushed forward until her hips met the pads and stood with my cock pressed to her ass. Kicking her feet wide, I bent over, covering her back with my much larger frame. "You're mine, mate. And after tonight, you'll never doubt me again."

* * *

Natalie

He stood behind me, his cock like a branding iron pressed in the crease of my bottom. Roark's fist was in my hair, pressing me slowly, gently, but inexorably forward until I leaned over the bench, my breasts swaying below me, the chain dangling low, nearly brushing the floor.

He kicked my legs wide, opening me to him, to whatever he wanted to do to me. "You're mine, mate. And after tonight, you'll never doubt me again."

I recognized this bench from my fantasy in the brides processing center. I knew my ankles would be tied, my wrists as well. I would be restrained and vulnerable. Weak. Completely under his control.

My pussy clenched, wetness coating my thighs even as fear reared its ugly head. Behind me was the man who wanted to remove his mark from my body. He wanted his gold, the symbol of his house, and the medallion, the only things that marked me as his, removed.

As much as my body longed for him, my heart literally ached with each beat. And my mind? The little girl who'd been left at boarding school like luggage, left alone at Christmas and abandoned to give birth and raise a son alone? She was in charge right now, and she didn't believe a word coming out of Roark's mouth.

"You'll walk away, Roark. Fine. Do it. Fuck me now and cut off your stupid chain in the morning."

CHAPTER 16

*N*atalie

GOD, it was stupid, but I couldn't seem to stop myself. I needed to push him, to make him hurt the way he was hurting me.

With a growl he held me down with one huge hand on the small of my back as he leaned over and secured my ankles to the base of the bench. That done, he walked around me and lowered my wrists into the leather restraints that were attached by slightly longer chains. I could move. I could lift my body until my back was horizontal to the floor, but no farther.

I expected him to walk behind me and stuff me with his cock. Instead, a sharp sting landed on my bare bottom.

Smack!
Smack!
Smack!

Fire spread through my body and I bucked and fought the restraints as he spanked me harder and faster.

"Who do you belong to?"

"Fuck you."

The spanking stopped and I bit my lip, fighting back tears. Had he given up so easily, then? Walked away, as I'd known he would, as everyone always did?

I felt something hard and small press against my bottom. When a strange wet warmth invaded my body there, I jerked. Slowly, very slowly, he pressed one finger into the forbidden area of my body, working past the tight ring of muscle. When he breeched me, I arched my back and cried out as he filled me, fucked me there with first one finger, then two. Legs spread wide, my pussy was empty and heavy, my breasts so engorged, so needy that they actually hurt.

Fingers buried in my body, his other hand landed on my bottom with a hard, sharp strike.

"You are mine. This ass is mine. Your pussy is mine. That little boy in the other room is mine. Your body is mine, *gara*. To fuck. To pleasure. To punish when you forget who you belong to." He carefully fucked my ass with his fingers as he spoke, pulling back and pushing forward, working me open in a way I'd never known before. I fought the heat that spread like wildfire through my blood at his words and his dominant touch. "Say you're mine. Call me master."

I shook my head, denying him, denying both of us. No. I would not make it that easy for him. I'd been so happy to see him on Earth, I'd welcomed him with open arms, ignored more than a year of pain, longing, hurt. That pain came roaring back now, refusing to be denied. "It's not that easy, Roark."

His palm landed on my ass and I startled forward. He followed me, pressing his fingers deep. "You're mine. Say it."

"Just let me go." The words were more sob than demand,

spoken by a scared little girl who'd never been chosen first, who'd never been loved the way she should have been, the way I would love Noah.

"Never." His fingers disappeared from me and he walked to a drawer near his massive bed. I watched out of the corner of my eye as he lifted something from the drawer, slid a large ring onto one of his fingers and returned to me. He held the item where I could see it, two spheres about the size of golf balls connected by a wire. "Do you know what these are?"

I knew, I remembered from the dream, but I shook my head and he walked behind me, pressing the first one at the opening of my bottom where his fingers had already prepared me. "These are stimspheres, *gara.* I can control them with the ring I just placed on my finger." He pushed first one, then the second inside me, filling me up as they popped past my inner muscle and began to vibrate deep inside my body. In the dream they were in my pussy, not my ass. But this, it was dark and carnal and, god, it felt so good. "They will make you come, mate, as many times as I want you to."

I yanked on the restraints that held my arms. The golden chain hanging from my breasts swung and pulled on my nipples and I bit back a groan of need. I would not give in so easily.

The stimspheres sparked, or fired, or whatever the hell they did, shooting sensation through every nerve ending in my body, traveling straight to my clit. The shock made me gasp as I rocked forward onto the bench, my knees collapsing.

"Who am I?"

"An asshole."

The stimspheres fired again, stronger this time, and I couldn't stop the moan that escaped my lips as my pussy clenched around empty space. I wanted his cock inside me, filling me, stretching me. I needed.

"Who am I?"

I couldn't speak, so I simply shook my head. His hand landed on my ass with a sharp sting, once, twice. The head of his huge cock slid to my core. He slipped just the tip inside me as the stimspheres fired in my backside again.

In an agony of need, I tried to shift back, to force my body onto his hard length, but the cuffs linked to my wrists prevented me from moving far enough to take him, to force him to fuck me. "Roark!"

"That's not my name, mate. Not when you are bent over and ripe for fucking. Who am I?"

Smack!

Smack!

Smack!

The spanking was whiplike, sharp and fast, and my entire body shivered as the sensation spread through me like lightning overcharging my nervous system.

I shuddered as he bent low over me, the tip of his cock just inside my body. His right hand traced the curve of my waist before dipping low, to my breasts, where he wrapped the thin chain around his fingers and tugged gently in a rhythm that made my breasts ache. I needed his mouth, his hands. More. I needed more.

"Who am I?"

"Just fuck me. Fuck me so I can cut off this stupid chain and go home."

"You are home."

Trapped by the chain pulling on my breasts, I could not shift position, not a single inch. His cock teased my entrance, denying me the one thing I needed. Him. Fucking me. Hard and fast. Making me scream. Making me come.

"Who am I?"

The word *master* was right there, on the tip of my tongue, but I would not give it to him. Not when he wanted to remove his chain, his mark, from my body. It was like giving a girl an engagement ring—no, a wedding ring—and then asking for the ring back. "No."

"So beautiful, mate. So stubborn." He whispered the words in my ear and I shuddered as he pressed forward inch by agonizing inch, his body covering mine, his cock stretching me open, filling me up. With the stimspheres still inside my body, I was full, so fucking full.

I dropped my head as he filled me, needing it. Needing him more than I wanted to admit. I was in love with the idiot, and he wanted to remove his mark from my body.

He pushed deep, until his balls hit my thighs and the tip of his cock pressed against my womb.

"I'm going to fill you with my seed, mate. I want to see you round with another child, a girl this time, with your blue eyes and fiery spirit."

Biting my lip at the picture he painted, I closed my eyes and fought back the tears. "I'm keeping the chain, Roark."

He stilled above me. "Why would you do that, Natalie? It's done nothing but cause you pain. My mark, the medallion, they've done nothing but place you in danger."

I processed his words and all the defiance drained from my muscles. "That's why you want to remove it?"

"Yes, *gara*. What did you think—" His voice trailed off and he moved his hips, pulled out and filled me with his cock, making us both groan. "Foolish female. You are mine. I will never let you go." He kissed the back of my shoulder. "I love you, Natalie. Forever."

The words made me wild. I'd waited a lifetime to hear them. Turning my head, I found his mouth, kissed him with every ounce of love and fear and desire and trust I could give him. "I love you. I'm not taking off your chain…Master."

Buried in my body, we were one, connected as he kissed me. I felt his love in the kiss. I allowed myself to feel it, to take a chance, to risk my heart one more time. When the kiss ended I looked up at him over my shoulder. "Don't break my heart again."

"You are my heart, Natalie Montgomery. You will never doubt my love again."

With a wicked grin he released the chain and lifted his body to stand behind me. The change in position gave him just a bit more length to push inside me and I whimpered as he pressed forward, driving deep. "Now, *gara*, who am I?"

"Master."

"What do you want from your master?"

"I want to come."

"Beg." He pulled out and thrust deep.

"Please."

The word became a chant as he fucked me. Hard and fast, the stimspheres shocked my system every time he pushed forward, driving into my wet core, making me frantic. The world faded to the thrust of his hips, the sound of wet fucking, the jolt of sensation from the stimspheres in my ass, the loud, wet sound of my pussy grabbing and milking his cock like a greedy fist.

He rode me hard, my body tied down. I could do nothing but accept every thrust, every stroke, every ounce of his power and need as he fucked me, filled me, made me beg.

My orgasm rose like a powerful wave boiling up from somewhere deep inside me I'd never allowed to break free. I shattered, breaking into a million pieces of pleasure as my pussy clenched and pulsed, my body arched and every nerve I had fired both pleasure and pain through my system.

Roark came, filling me with his seed, the jerking of his cock setting me off again.

When it was over, I collapsed, not even trying to assist

him as he released me from the restraints and carried me to his bed. He settled me beside him, tucking us both under the warm cover.

"*Gara*, never talk about leaving me again."

Nestled safely in his arms, I didn't have the strength left for fear. "The chain stays, Roark. You're mine."

He chuckled softly as he rolled me onto my back and settled his body between the cradle of my hips. He was hard and ready, and when he shifted his body, entering me in one slow, steady push, I opened my legs wider, welcoming him. "All right, *gara*. If you insist. You are mine. Removing the adornment will not change that, nor will it lessen the risk from those who want to hurt me."

"I insist." I lifted my arms, wrapping them around his head to pull him down for a proper kiss.

He kissed me, long and unhurried as his cock fucked me with a slow, languorous rhythm that made my heart throb almost as much as my aching pussy did. "You are my heart, mate. If they hurt you, they hurt me."

"Then don't let them hurt me."

He growled, thrusting deep. "Never again."

I kissed him, kissed away the pain and fear of the past, for both of us. "I want a little girl." Shifting my hips, I rocked into him. "I want forever."

"Forever won't be long enough."

I smiled as he fucked me, arched off the bed when the orgasm claimed me, when he used the stimspheres to make me come again and again. I whimpered as he filled me with his seed, greedy for more, for a daughter to love. This was my future, my home.

FIND YOUR MATCH!

YOUR mate is out there. Take the test today and discover your perfect match. Are you ready for a sexy alien mate (or two)?

VOLUNTEER NOW!
interstellarbridesprogram.com

WANT MORE?

Sign up for Grace's VIP Reader list at
http://freescifiromance.com

Read the first chapter of MATING FEVER:

Megan Simmons, Medical Station, Battleship Karter, *Sector 437*

I was being kissed. And carried. Literally lifted off my feet and a hot, very insistent mouth was on mine. We were moving but I didn't know to where. I didn't care. I just wanted to be kissed.

Hot. Deep. Lush. My body responded instantly. My pussy became wet, my nipples hardened when a growl rumbled deep in his chest. I felt it as much as heard the carnal sound.

All at once, I was pushed against a wall and I felt every hard inch of him pressing into me. He was big. So big that I felt the thick outline of his cock pressing high against my belly.

"Mine," he said, his voice a harsh rasp. His lips only lifted enough for him to breathe that one word, but I felt it all the way to my toes.

Yes. I had no problem agreeing with that. I had no idea who this guy was or why he was kissing me, but I didn't care. I wanted him with a desperation I'd never known.

Through our clothes I felt his heat. It was as if he had a fever, his body raging with a need for me that all but consumed him, turned him into something dark and primitive.

"Yes, yours," I whispered.

His hands slid down my body, down my *bare* body. Wait. I was naked. *He* was dressed. I should stop him, but why? It felt too damn good.

I didn't need my clothes. I needed him to remove his.

He stepped back and I was able to see he wore the uniform of a Coalition fighter, and he filled it out so beautifully. I couldn't, though, see his face. Why? Why couldn't I see who was making me so needy?

His hands went to his pants, opened them and pulled out his cock. Whoa, now that was a monster cock. Long and thick with a broad head, I licked my lips with an eagerness to taste him.

What the hell was wrong with me? I didn't salivate after a stranger's cock.

Until now.

"Mine." There was that one word, witty dialogue again, but my body responded as if he'd just whispered a hundred and one erotic, naughty deeds he was going to do to me. He reached for my wrists, lifted my hands to his lips where he kissed the metal I now noticed circled my wrists.

Atlan mating cuffs.

Holy shit.

Fascinated, I stared as he traced the intricate design chiseled into the metal with his tongue. I couldn't look away from the way the metal about my wrists glinted in the light. Gold and silver tones combined to make beautiful, wide bracelets. I'd seen Atlan mating cuffs before, knew that if I turned my attention to his wrists, he would be wearing a matching pair. They felt far heavier than I'd ever imagined, significant. He acted as if they were. His body curled over mine, so possessive, as if I truly belonged to him. He kissed the palms of my hands and I felt an amazing sense of power rush through me as this giant beast of a man worshipped my skin, kissed me with a featherlight touch as if I were fragile china.

As a woman, I should be offended by his blatant claim. I was a battle-hardened warrior and could take care of myself. But this...this...gentle giant was unmaking me.

My body quivered like a plucked guitar string and I closed my eyes as he raised my hands above my head. Somehow I knew what was coming, knew there was a hook in the wall above my head, knew that if I let him raise my hands, I'd be bound, trapped.

Instead of running, screaming, kicking, demanding to be freed, I lifted my arms and thrust out my chest, eager for the roughness of his tongue on my nipples. This body was his. He could have me as long as he put that perfect cock inside me.

With my hands locked above me, he stepped back and stripped out of his pants. Naked and glorious, he was huge, his eyes peering at me through the darkness with a strange animal heat. His large hand gripped the base of his cock and he began to stroke up and down the length, bringing about a shiny pearl of fluid from the slit at the tip. I couldn't miss the matching cuffs about his own wrists below the cut of his uniform jacket. "Mine. Mate."

I watched as he continued to stroke himself. "That cock is mine, beast. Give it to me."

Whoa! Where had that sassy wench come from? I seemed to have no control over this body, or this sharp tongue, but the beast before me didn't seem to mind. He chuckled before dropping to his knees. Before I could blink, he'd lifted my thighs to rest on his shoulders and his tongue was inside me.

"Yes!" I locked my ankles behind his head and held him to me. The shudder that moved through his powerful frame made me groan. His mouth was hot, so hot. But I wanted more. I needed him inside me, stretching me open, filling me up.

He was mine. He had to be mine.

The beast worked me with his tongue until I couldn't think, my pussy so wet and swollen that I actually ached there, my pulse moving through me like a blowtorch. He was big and powerful, definitely one dominant male, but I had the power here. Only I could tame his beast. He would be mine forever. Forever. And he needed me, needed me to soothe his beast. My body, my acceptance, was crucial to his very survival.

He stood, cupped my breasts, played with them. I reveled in the feel of his calloused touch. He wasn't gentle. No, his thumbs and forefingers tweaked my already tight tips, bringing about a delicious moan and the arching of my back.

Gripping behind my knee, he lifted me up so our bodies were aligned. I no longer felt the floor beneath my bare feet; I was supported between his heated body and the cool wall.

"Mate," he growled, running his tongue along my collarbone, tasting me. Marking me.

"You're mine. All mine," I replied.

When he slid the head of his cock through my slick folds, perhaps to test my readiness, I whimpered. "Yes. Do it."

"Mine."

Oh yes. I needed him to fill me up. God, was he trying to kill me with lust? "Mine. Mine. Mine. You're mine."

"Beg," his growl was nothing less than an order.

My eyes flew open to find him watching me intently, even lost in the throes of mating fever, his beast wanted to dominate me, force me to surrender. And fuck me, if that didn't make me hotter. I couldn't catch my breath. My heart was going to burst from behind my rib cage and explode like a firework.

"Please," I breathed when his cock settled at my eager entrance.

"Mine 'til death."

Those were heavy words. Like marriage vows, but insanely more serious. There was no annulment between mates, no divorce. This was a bond on an elemental level. I knew that by fucking him I was more than just sating the man. As he said, I was soothing his beast. He would be bound to me forever, a possessive, arrogant, protective, dominant alpha male. I could recite dozens of reasons I should turn him away, refuse his claim, choose someone else.

But I wanted him. Only him. I loved the demanding, dominant lover. I wanted him fucking me so hard I wouldn't remember my own name. I didn't want to think, I wanted to feel. I didn't want to worry about taking care of myself. For once in my life, I was going to give up control. I was going to let him take care of me. I was going to *submit.*

My body melted at the thought. Yes. I needed him to take control, to force my mind to stop whirring and churning, just to let me feel.

"Fill me up. Please." I shifted my hips and had him slide into me about an inch. Just that little bit opened me, stretched me. I knew having that entire cock inside me would almost split me open. I should be running away, not settling myself on him further.

"Now," I said, my hands in fists above the cuffs. I was

spread before him like a feast. "Now," I repeated and cried out when he slid all the way in one long, smooth, hard stroke.

"Mine," he growled.

I threw my head back as he stretched me open. The pleasure-pain triggered my first orgasm as he stared down into my eyes like a hunter, watching me, holding my gaze as my pussy clamped down on him like a fist, pulsing and gripping him as my entire body shook.

God. More. I needed more... Pulling out, he slammed deep in one hard thrust and my back hit the wall.

"Miss Simmons." I heard a woman's voice coming from far away, but ignored it as my beast filled me up with a harsh growl.

Yes, it was so good. I loved his cock. Needed it. He pulled back, filled me again...yes!

"Miss Simmons!" That voice again. Insistent. Exasperated. Whoever she was, couldn't she see I was a bit busy here?

I shook my head, focused on feeling the wall at my back, huge Atlan hands on my hips, his cock between my thighs. The sharp pinch of the cuffs forcing my body to take what he gave me, to take the pleasure, the thrill of danger that I felt placing my body under his command. Of being his. Totally. Completely. His.

His giant cock withdrew. Thrust deep. God. So big. So hard. An edge of pain that I loved.

"Megan?" That woman's voice again, sounding irritated this time. I ignored her. I didn't want her. I wanted him. His cock. His huge hands. His heat.

"Megan! Soldier, snap out of it!"

Oh, the voice was getting bitchy now, but I didn't care. I shook my head and bit my lip as my mate fucked me hard. I was going to come again. God, I was so close—

"Prepare the neural stimulant. She's not coming out of the testing."

Testing?

That one word triggered a memory. The doctor. The ship. Once my mind started down that slippery slope, the rest faded. *He* faded. I tried to hold on to him, onto the pleasure, but the feelings drifted from my mind like sand being carried away by a windstorm. I opened my eyes, blinked. There was no sexy alpha male fucking me up against a wall like I was his favorite treat. There was no male at all.

Which pretty much summed up my life lately. At least in the sex department. I was surrounded by men on the battleship, thousands of them. But I hadn't had sex in over a year, and my body was not satisfied with the small taste I'd just been given. I wanted more. Which was just my luck, because I wasn't going to be getting any action. Not for a few more days at least.

"Oh, good." The woman's voice belonged to Doctor Moor. I recognized her dark brown hair and kind face hovering over me. She was an Atlan female, which meant she looked human, mostly, except she was well over six feet tall with shoulders broader than most football players. The Atlan Warlords were big men, so I wasn't surprised that the women were sized to match. She was dressed in the usual green doctor's uniform, her hair cut short in a pixie style that made her big brown eyes practically jump out of her face. She was gorgeous. But more importantly, she was kind. Which was why I'd come to her for the Interstellar Brides Program testing. I was not about to let one of the Prillon doctors loom over me while I was having an intense sexual experience dream, possibly involving one of their kin.

No way. Not happening. Doctor Moor suited me just fine. *And so had that dream.*

Looking around, I recognized the dark green stripes lining the walls, the exam chairs that looked like the ones I used to sit in at the dentist's office when I was a kid. Lying here, I felt small. These things were built to hold huge alien warriors, Atlans and Prillons being the biggest, most close to seven feet tall. And in beast mode? The Atlans topped out at eight or nine feet, like the *Incredible Hulk* minus the green skin. They were huge, brutally efficient killers, and sexy as hell. At least to me. Nothing made me happier than seeing a battalion of Atlan Warlords swarm the battlefield around me and literally rip enemy Hive soldiers in half with their bare hands.

So I had a wee bit of a violent nature. I'd made peace with that side of myself a long time ago when I joined the Army. Not everyone was cut out for flower garlands and peace protests. No one in my family, at least. But I was more than willing to fight and die to protect those who were. Put a gun, or an ion blaster, in my hand and turn me loose on anything evil. Terrorists on Earth. Hive drones in space. They were all the same to me. Evil was evil. Fighting them made me feel powerful. Made me feel like part of the family. My dad and both my brothers went into the military. Therefore, I went into the military, even though I was a *girl. A half-black, half-Irish mutt from Boston.*

I could pull the trigger on my rifle just fine.

I was also the only one who'd transferred from the Earth army to join the Coalition Fleet. Not that it made a difference to my mother. I'd fought the Hive for almost two years now—my term was almost up—and seen some seriously insane shit. I wasn't a weak girl. I was a powerful woman who not only stood up to the Hive, but baited them, trapped them. Killed them. Killed their leaders. Sneaked behind enemy lines and lured the Integration Units away from their protective Hive Soldiers and Scouting units. We'd been targeting the Integration Units, the Hive responsible for torturing and assimilating their captives into the Hive collective mind, for months. But now I had bigger fish to fry. Top Secret fish.

We were hunting their Core communication units, the Nexus Units. A few days ago, we'd almost had one. But our intel was bad. They were guarded by a full dozen Hive Soldier class warriors, big, strong bastards that were hard to kill. The last op had almost killed me, and the Soldier unit had taken out the rest of the warriors assigned to the Op before I could do anything to stop them. We'd managed to get to one of the smaller Nexus creatures. Killed him. But his communications unit had been fried. Worthless. Three dead Coalition warriors...and all for nothing.

I couldn't live with that, which was why I was going back down there. Tomorrow. The I.C., or Intelligence Core, the elite Coalition minds that ran the intelligence arm of this war, were assigning me a team of five highly trained killers to take into that canyon tomorrow. This time, I wouldn't fail. My last mission would not be a failure. I'd hear my mother's disapproving voice in my head forever if I walked away now. *"Why can't you be tough, like your brothers?"* and *"Stop your crying, little bitch. You sound like a girl."* And my personal favorite, *"Jesus, Mary and Joseph, you never shoulda been born into this family."*

The doctor circled me as the memories flooded my mind. Not of rough hands and desire, but of slaps across the face when my mother was drunk, and words that cut so deep I didn't think my heart would ever stop bleeding.

My dad was a big, powerful black man, fierce and protective. He'd loved us all, when he was home, and I'd loved him with a fierceness that still filled my spine with steel. My mother had been better then, happy. But he died when I was nine and she never recovered, started drinking whiskey like it was water, and the more she drank, the meaner she got. My dad was dead.

Had been for a long time. My brothers were tough assholes, still on Earth, still serving their country. I had no idea where they were now. Afghanistan? Syria? Africa? Hell, they could be shitting ice in Antarctica for all I knew. I got a message from my youngest brother about twice a year, letting me know they were all still alive. Even *Shirley.* Shirley Simmons. "Mother" was not a word I liked to use these days and he knew that.

I surrounded myself with strength. Tough men. Thick armor. Powerful weapons. I trained to keep both my mind and my body strong. I was almost six-foot tall. I wasn't used to feeling small or vulnerable, but sitting in this damn chair made me feel like a child-sized doll. I was several inches taller than the average woman on Earth, but here? Here I was like a toddler sitting at the grownup table swinging two feet that didn't reach the floor.

Fortunately, the commanders in the Coalition Fleet knew how to take advantage of my size and stealth. And my team's mission tomorrow was proof of that. Sometimes, it was better to be the scorpion than the lion. Small but deadly. That was my motto. Hell, that was pretty much the motto of all humans out here in deep space. We weren't as big as some of the alien races, but we were mean as fuck when we had to be. It was a matter of pride. To me, it was my personal mission.

"Are you with me, Megan?" The doctor leaned over, shining one of those stupid bright lights right into my eyes and I winced. Too bright.

"Unfortunately." I wanted that big man, his huge cock. I wanted to feel beautiful and feminine and desired. Instead, I had one more mission, one more op wearing that heavy armor and helmet, coated in grime, killing things. One. More.

Embrace the suck.

That was practically my family motto, and I'd learned it

well. Those three words got me through grueling hours of training, pain, and being stranded in hostile territory more than once in the last two years. I'd been cold, hot, starving, coated in sweat, blood, and every other body fluid I could imagine, and some I never dreamed of until I came out here into space. Outer fucking space. When I stopped to think about the fact that I was floating in a tin can in a galaxy far, far away, I still freaked. So, I tried not to think about it.

The doctor clicked off the penlight and I could see again. I looked up into her face in time to see her nod with a smile. "Good. I didn't want to have to inject you with neural stimulants."

She held up a small green cylinder I knew from previous experience could sting worse than any needle back home. Sure, there was no needle. But that just meant they forced the substance through your skin with something else. I didn't know how they worked. Didn't want to know. "No thanks. Keep that thing away from me."

The doctor chuckled and handed off the cylinder to an assistant who took the dosing unit and hurried away like he was intruding on a highly personal conversation. Which he was. And that thought brought me back to reality faster than anything else. I was very much awake now. No dream guy. No dream cock. No taunting or teasing or edging. No incredible orgasm.

I was in the brides testing room in the medical wing of the Battleship Karter. Damn. I very much preferred to be back in fantasyland with a very dominant male who knew what to do with his hands, and his cock. It had been far, far too long since I had anything besides my fingers between my legs.

"Did I scream?" I could feel my cheeks heat. "Please, tell me I didn't scream." I'd kill myself with my own ion blaster if

189

the males in the medical floor heard me screaming with an orgasm based on a dream.

"You didn't scream." She grinned then and gave me a conspiratorial wink. "I've never been tested, but every bride who has always has a very arousing experience."

She was a few years older than me. She might not have been tested through the brides program like I just had, but with the gold cuffs about her wrists, she was obviously mated to an Atlan, so she knew quite a bit about bossy Atlan males. And big cocks. And, based on my dream, on the cuffs I'd worn, and the giant-sized man fucking my brains out, I was going to be matched to both.

The thought of an Atlan mate made me shiver and my pussy clenched as heat flooded me. I should be surprised that my deepest self would want one of those huge, brutal warriors, but somehow I wasn't. Over the past two years of fighting alongside the Coalition forces, I'd encountered many Atlans and they were all over the top. Dominant. Controlling. Annoying. They had nothing against females, weren't disrespectful or chauvinistic. The opposite, in fact. They just took *alpha male* to the extreme. Protective. Demanding. Merciless.

I shivered, tingles running over my skin at that one word. Merciless. They showed no mercy to their enemies. And I was shocked to discover, I wanted none in bed.

Read more now!

DO YOU LOVE AUDIOBOOKS?

Grace Goodwin's books are now available as
audiobooks…everywhere.

CONNECT WITH GRACE

Interested in joining my not-so-secret Facebook Sci-Fi Squad? Get excerpts, cover reveals and sneak peeks before anyone else. Be part of a closed Facebook group that shares pictures and fun news. JOIN Here: http://bit.ly/SciFiSquad

All of Grace's books can be read as sexy, stand-alone adventures. Her Happily-Ever-Afters are always free from cheating because she writes Alpha males, NOT Alphaholes. (You can figure that one out.) But be careful...she likes her heroes hot and her love scenes hotter. You have been warned...

www.gracegoodwin.com
gracegoodwinauthor@gmail.com

ABOUT GRACE

Grace Goodwin is a *USA Today* and international bestselling author of Sci-Fi & Paranormal romance. Grace believes all women should be treated like princesses, in the bedroom and out of it, and writes love stories where men know how to make their women feel pampered, protected and very well taken care of. Grace hates the snow, loves the mountains (yes, that's a problem) and wishes she could simply download the stories out of her head instead of being forced to type them out. Grace lives in the western US and is a full-time writer, an avid romance reader and an admitted caffeine addict.

Her Viken Mates

Fighting For Their Mate

Her Rogue Mates

Claimed By The Vikens

Interstellar Brides®: The Colony

Surrender to the Cyborgs

Mated to the Cyborgs

Cyborg Seduction

Her Cyborg Beast

Cyborg Fever

Rogue Cyborg

Interstellar Brides®: The Virgins

The Alien's Mate

Claiming His Virgin

His Virgin Mate

His Virgin Bride

Other Books

Their Conquered Bride

Wild Wolf Claiming: A Howl's Romance